EVIL INTENT

DI SARA RAMSEY
BOOK TWENTY

M A COMLEY

ACKNOWLEDGMENTS

Special thanks as always go to @studioenp for their superb cover design expertise.

My heartfelt thanks go to my wonderful editor Emmy, and my proofreader Joseph for spotting all the lingering nits.

Thank you also to my amazing ARC Group who help to keep me sane during this process.

To Mary, gone, but never forgotten. I hope you found the peace you were searching for my dear friend. I miss you each and every day.

ALSO BY M A COMLEY

Seeking Justice (a 15,000 word novella)

Caring For Justice (a 24,000 word novella)

Savage Justice (a 17,000 word novella)

Justice at Christmas #2 (a 15,000 word novella)

Gone in Seconds (Justice Again series #1)

Ultimate Dilemma (Justice Again series #2)

Shot of Silence (Justice Again series #3)

Taste of Fury (Justice Again series #4)

Crying Shame (Justice Again series #5)

See No Evil (Justice Again #6)

To Die For (DI Sam Cobbs #1)

To Silence Them (DI Sam Cobbs #2)

To Make Them Pay (DI Sam Cobbs #3)

To Prove Fatal (DI Sam Cobbs #4)

To Condemn Them (DI Sam Cobbs #5)

To Punish Them (DI Sam Cobbs #6)

To Entice Them (DI Sam Cobbs #7)

To Control Them (DI Sam Cobbs #8)

To Endanger Lives (DI Sam Cobbs #9)

To Hold Responsible (DI Sam Cobbs #10)

Forever Watching You (DI Miranda Carr thriller)

Wrong Place (DI Sally Parker thriller #1)

No Hiding Place (DI Sally Parker thriller #2)

Cold Case (DI Sally Parker thriller#3)

Deadly Encounter (DI Sally Parker thriller #4)

Lost Innocence (DI Sally Parker thriller #5)

Goodbye My Precious Child (DI Sally Parker #6)

The Missing Wife (DI Sally Parker #7)

A Time For Change (A Sweet Romance)

High Spirits

The Temptation series (Romantic Suspense/New Adult Novellas)

Past Temptation

Lost Temptation

Clever Deception (co-written by Linda S Prather)

Tragic Deception (co-written by Linda S Prather)

Sinful Deception (co-written by Linda S Prather)

PROLOGUE

"She's an absolute treasure, mostly. I don't hear a peep out of her after her head hits the pillow, so to speak. When I get up during the night, I check on her out of habit more than anything. She's rarely awake, though. On the odd occasion when she does wake up, she's sitting in her cot playing with her teddy," Eve said, proudly puffing out her chest. She leaned forward and gave her daughter, Mia, a small piece of her banana, in the hope that it would satisfy her needs until they got home in about an hour.

This was only their second trip to the mother and baby group. It had taken her longer than anticipated to get out of the house and back into the swing of meeting new people. She'd always been a confident member of society, but something had changed within her once she'd given birth to Mia six months before. She was still trying to figure out what that specifically was. One thing was certain, she was a great protector of her new daughter. At least Covid had taught her how to protect her and her family from unwanted germs. She was clued up there and rarely let anyone else near her baby, for fear of someone giving Mia a nasty infection that might be incredibly hard to get rid of. She'd seen the effects that Long Covid had on a person, one who was in their mid-thirties, in the shape of her sister, Amelia. She had been hospitalised during lockdown for four weeks and had suffered with Long Covid ever since, susceptible to breathing issues and chest infections that meant she was no longer capable of holding down a job.

Amelia detested being on benefits, but she saw it as a necessary evil. How else was she expected to cover the exorbitant bills facing everyone living in the entire UK right now?

Eve and Paul were struggling. There was talk of her going back to work soon, and even asking Amelia to look after Mia during the day for a few hours. Her sister was still debating whether that was a good option for her or not, in light of her poor health. Would it be fair on either of them? Mia had become such a demanding little soul in the past few weeks. Amelia had voiced her concerns, and Eve had selfishly and hastily pushed them aside.

She drifted back into the conversation she was having with the other mothers, comparing each of their babies' sleep patterns, some more vocal than others, expressing their points of view. Eve didn't feel the need to comment further, she was more than happy with the way her parenting skills had developed since she'd left hospital. The birth itself had been traumatic. Eight hours of exhaustingly pushing and bearing down had resulted in Eve pleading with them to do a C-section; she had been convinced there was something wrong with Mia inside the womb and she had been proved right. The umbilical cord was found to be tightening around Mia's neck. Paul had begged the nursing staff to do all they could to save their precious baby, and Mia had been born, happy and at a healthy weight of eight pounds and twelve ounces.

Eve had remained in hospital for four days. Having the operation instead of going down the natural route had devastated her, knocked her physically and mentally, and she had struggled to understand why. Every time she glanced down at the perfect bundle she was holding, gazing into Mia's bright-blue eyes, she realised how lucky she was to have her. The woman opposite her on the ward had given birth to a stillborn daughter, which had torn Eve's heart out the minute she had heard the news. She found it near impossible to put herself in the woman's position, going through nine long months of pregnancy, only to have your baby taken from you by God. The thing that perturbed Eve the most about the situation was the way the medical staff had kept the poor woman on the maternity ward.

Of course, she realised it would have been a tough call either way, but it didn't stop her considering how the woman must have felt, surrounded by the hustle and bustle of a maternity ward, alive with new life and all that entailed when she had obviously reached rock bottom.

"What about feeding times, Eve?" Claudine asked, interrupting her thoughts.

"She's a greedy monkey, I never know if she's had enough," Eve replied. She ran a finger around Mia's face and smiled when her bundle of joy strained. "I think someone is in the process of filling her nappy."

"I find they always do it at the most inopportune moment, don't you?" Lynne said.

"It's what babies do, I guess," Eve countered. She'd had enough. She needed to get out of there, be on her own with her daughter for some much-needed bonding time, making the most of her husband working away from home. He tended to take over most duties when he was around and not working. Eve wasn't entirely sure how she felt about him doing that just yet. Sometimes she felt left out, even though she tried not to show it, giving the game away to Paul and the other members of their extended family who dared to monopolise her daughter's time instead of her. She needed to learn how to share, which was becoming increasingly difficult as her bond with Mia grew.

The group chat came to an end a few minutes later, and the women drifted off. She decided it would be better to visit the loo before she and Mia set off, to change Mia's full nappy and wash banana mush off her hands and face. *Happy baby, deliriously happy mother*, wasn't that how the saying went? She remembered reading it somewhere in one of those supposedly helpful books that set out to prepare new mothers with what to look forward to once their offspring entered the world. Most of what the authors had to say went over her head, she'd struggled to take it all in during the months leading up to the birth, and afterwards, well, time just wasn't on her side, not at all.

When Eve emerged from the toilet only the staff were around. "Sorry if I'm holding you up, that wasn't my intention at all. Mia filled her nappy, and I thought it would be better changing her now than when I got home."

Becky, one of the co-owners, rested a hand on Eve's arm. "You're not putting us out at all, we won't be ready to leave for another hour or so yet, so don't even think that. Is Mia okay now?"

They both glanced down at Mia who was staring back at them, nibbling the ear of her fluffy teddy.

"She's perfect, happy as a pig in muck," Eve replied. "Ouch, I can't believe I used that analogy."

They both chuckled.

"Do you need anything else before you head off?" Becky asked.

"No, nothing. Thanks for putting up with us today, we'll be back next week."

"No problem, we're here when you need us. Don't ever think you're alone on this incredible journey. Most mothers come a few times and then drop out, believing they can cope on their own with the new baby, only to find the opposite is true in some cases. Being a new mum can be a very lonely experience to some mothers."

"Oh, why do you think that is?" Eve asked, intrigued.

"Hormones mostly. Giving birth is one of life's great mysteries. What appears to be an easy task for some can be ultra-traumatic to others. Every mother and her relationship with her child will be different, there's no one size fits all, as you've no doubt realised by now."

"I have. Just getting involved in the conversation today, everyone sharing their own experiences, and I noticed the comparisons vary so much from mother to mother."

"As I said," Becky began, "one size rarely fits all, everyone's experience and circumstances will be different. We can dish out all the well-meaning advice under the sun, but it won't match everyone's needs."

"I suppose that's right. I must admit, I did find myself getting a touch uptight when Francis tried ramming it down my throat what I should do when Mia cries. It's something I need to work out for myself. Mia and I have a special bond. I guess all mothers will tell you that, won't they?"

"Not all. Some who have experienced post-natal depression will tell you how difficult it was bonding with their baby. That's when doctors and medicines come into their own. To return the woman's body back to near normal as quickly as possible after the birth, to give the mothers and babies every conceivable fighting chance."

"Yes, Claudine was telling me the other day how much the medication her doctor had put her on had saved her."

Becky nodded. "Claudine is a totally different person to the one who showed up here a few months back. She has really come out of her shell in the past month or so, since the tablets have worked their way into her system. Anyway, I can't stand around here gossiping all day, not that I've divulged any secrets, I wouldn't do that. We're all here for you, should you need any extra advice. Have a brief look at the noticeboard on your way out, there are several coffee mornings and other craft groups for you to get involved in, when, or if, you feel the time is right."

"Thanks, Becky. I'll stop off and have a look on my way out. Congratulations on servicing the needs of the public so well. Oh my, did I really say that? That sounded so formal. I drifted back to my previous career then, for a second or two."

"What career did you have, and is there any chance of you going back to it soon?"

"I was a wedding planner in my former life, pre-Mia days. And truthfully, I'm not sure if I could take the pressure. It was pretty stressful most days, dealing with harassed couples, sorting out what they needed for their big day."

"Rather you than me. My hubby and I eloped to Gretna Green, just took our nearest and dearest with us. The money we saved ended up being put down on our house as a huge deposit. I can never understand the need for couples to fork out twenty grand or more on a single day, that has never sat well with me at all."

"Twenty grand? Most people end up spending double that these days."

"Bloody hell, there you go then, I rest my case. It's deplorable. A single day..." Becky wagged her finger. "No, I should keep my mouth shut on the topic, each to their own, and we won't even mention the divorce statistics, will we?"

Eve cringed. "Yes, it's no joke these days. We're now a disposable society, aren't we? Getting rid of unwanted possessions, which sometimes include our other halves. Makes me appreciate my husband more, that's for sure. He's working extra hours at the moment, keen not to have me return to work."

"He sounds like a decent chap. Not every man would put himself out like that. Most of them think it's a doddle bringing up a baby, being on call twenty-four-seven, three hundred and sixty-five days a year."

"Thankfully, Paul isn't like that at all. He's always putting Mia and me first, in all his decisions."

"That's great to hear. He's a keeper, hon. We'll see you again next week then. If you need anything in the meantime, don't hesitate to ring us."

"You're too kind, thanks, Becky. Enjoy the rest of your day."

"You, too. What's on the agenda?"

"As it's a nice day, I bundled together a small picnic, thought we'd go for a stroll around the park and have our lunch there."

"Go, enjoy yourselves. I'm a tad envious hearing that, I haven't had a picnic in yonks. They used to be a regular occurrence in our house years ago. Funny how we forget to do things that give us such pleasure sometimes."

"Finding the time in your hectic day must be a chore. Put a date on your calendar and stick to it, that was how I used to plan my week when I was working."

"Sounds like a good idea, thanks for the heads-up. Have fun at the park with this special lady." Becky touched Mia's cheek and then waved goodbye and headed back into the room where the meeting had taken place.

Eve used a wet wipe to wash Mia's cheek and pushed the pram out of the main door, which was propped open for ease, and into the bright sunshine. "Looks like we chose the perfect day to set off on our exciting adventure, little one."

Mia gurgled and sucked on her teddy's ear. Eve pushed her daughter past the row of posh town houses towards Aylestone Park on the edge of the city centre. It was where she and Paul had carried out their dating most days. He'd had a sweet Labrador when she'd first met him that tragically got run over one day. He was so broken-hearted that the thought of them replacing Coco had never cropped up.

She strolled through the park and ventured up near the top, where the picnic benches were situated. Luckily, at this time of year, the students from the nearby schools and colleges were all caught up in their exams. She unloaded the picnic she had cobbled together that morning and fed Mia in between nibbling on her Granary ham and cheese sandwich. Several birds fluttered around them, hoping to pick up the odd crumb or two. She propped Mia up in her pram to see the spectacle of the tiny birds edging closer to the table and then retreating every time Eve dared to raise her hand to feed either Mia or herself. It was lovely, the perfect day being surrounded by nature in all its glory. A few dogs barked in the distance as they chased each other around the small clump of trees in the dappled shade they cast.

Several couples, young and old, wandered past them and said good morning.

Replete, Eve packed up all their rubbish, choosing to take it home with her rather than litter the park unnecessarily. She then pushed Mia around the path to the exit at the rear that led through to the small estate. She decided to take the scenic route and turned right instead of going left like she usually did. The sun was heating up now. Eve raised her head and bathed in the warmth on her skin. Her mobile rang, interrupting her peace. She debated whether to ignore it or not, but when she saw who was calling, she dived in and answered it.

"Hello, Paul. To what do we owe the pleasure? I thought you were travelling up to Newcastle today."

"I'm already here. I set off really early from Nottingham and got here at around eleven. How did it go at the mother and baby group this morning? I was thinking about you both during the journey."

"It was great. I had a fabulous chat with Becky afterwards, she's a co-owner there. She's lovely and made me feel really welcome. Actually, they all did, considering it was only my second visit."

"That's great news. And what are you up to now?"

"We're winding our way back home after having a sneaky picnic at the park."

"Hey, why not? I take it the sun's out where you are? It's cold, damp and miserable up here today. It's supposed to brighten up later this afternoon. I can't wait. All this rain certainly affects your mood."

"How's work going? Any new major leads on the table yet?"

"A few. I've already reached my target for the month with the sale I brokered yesterday. I'm aiming for the bonus now, hence my decision to venture up this far, now that the area isn't being covered."

"When are they likely to fill the post up that way?"

"Interviews are being held next week, so they should have someone in place sooner rather than later. I know it's a pain in the arse, me being away, but the possibility of getting that bonus before the quarter is up is something we need to cling on to, love. Sorry."

"Don't be. Needs must. I know you don't want to be away from us longer than is necessary. Did you hear on the news that the mortgage rates have gone up again?"

"I did. I heard it but tried to ignore it at the same time. That's the one thing that's really crippling us at the moment.

It's rising at a horrendous rate. Although, saying that, we've still got it good compared to when our parents first started out. They made a point of telling me last week they had to put up with fifteen percent mortgage rates. Ours is around the five percent mark at the moment, dread to think what sort of position that would put us in if we were lumbered with those kinds of rates."

"It doesn't bear thinking about, does it? Everything is skyrocketing at the moment, and all they keep blaming it on is the war in the Ukraine."

"Yeah, easy to blame Putin. I think it has more to do with Brexit, but what do I know? Anyway, how the hell did we get onto the subject of politics? I try to avoid the topic as much as possible."

"That makes two of us. You'd better get on and try and acquire another deal or two by the end of the day."

"Yes, if it will keep the wolves from the door for longer. I'll give you a call later this evening, at around seven-thirty, how's that?"

"Perfect. I'll have bathed Mia and put her to bed by then. Have a productive day, and thanks for thinking of us, Paul."

"No problem. You're always on my mind, Eve. Give my special little girl a big sloppy kiss from her dad."

"I'll be sure to do that. Love you."

"Ditto. We'll do something nice at the weekend, I promise."

She laughed. "I'll hold you to that, as long as it doesn't involve going down that blasted zip line in Wales again."

"Ha, no chance. Not that it wasn't fun to feel the wind blowing through our hair last year."

"I could have done without me being five months pregnant when we went."

"Ouch, yes, I didn't think about that at the time. You came out of it unscathed, though, we both did."

"Barely, but that's another story. Go, earn us some dosh."

"I'm going. Speak to you later."

Eve blew him a kiss and tucked her phone into her jacket pocket. Rapid footsteps pounded behind her, and a thud smacked onto the back of her head.

Everything went black as she tumbled to the pavement.

CHAPTER 1

*S*ara braced herself for the backlash she knew was coming her way by placing a hand over her eyes and chewing on the inside of her cheek as she waited for the phone to be answered. "Hi, Lorraine, I thought I'd check in. See how you're feeling now that you're back at work."

"Right, let's get one thing straight. I've told you a million —no, correct that—a gazillion times already that I'm fine and dandy. Everything is okay with me and there is absolutely no need for you to keep pestering me night and day."

"In my defence, I've only rung you twice since you returned to work. Pardon me for caring."

Lorraine huffed out an impatient breath. "I warned you that you would be putting our friendship on the line if you tried mollycoddling me."

"I repeat, I'm not, and as far as I'm concerned, I have never tried to mollycoddle you, as if you'd let me anyway. Give me a break, Lorraine. If you'd prefer me to back off, I'll do it willingly, but don't come knocking on my door in a couple of months, accusing me of being an insensitive bitch when I don't bother checking in on you, got that?"

"Received and understood. Now, I have a mountain of work to catch up on. As you're probably aware, when a perfectionist takes enforced time off from their daily routine, they invariably have a few days of chaos to overcome once they return to work full time."

"I can imagine. Are you up to tackling the said mountain?"

"Jesus Christ, what have I just spent the last few minutes trying to tell you? Rewording your concerns isn't the answer, Sara, now fuck off and leave me to get back to my work before you and I fall out, big time."

Sara held the phone away from her ear, glared at it and growled. She stopped short of voicing the fierce retort teetering on the tip of her tongue and decided it would be in both of their interests to end the call.

She turned her attention to the paperwork littering her desk which mainly consisted of tying up the loose ends to the last couple of cases she and the team had solved, including the one where Hanson had kidnapped and tortured her dear friend, Lorraine, the Home Office patholo-gist, the same person who had just pulled her to pieces over the phone.

A knock on the door interrupted her thoughts a few minutes later. "Come in."

Her partner, Carla Jameson, popped her head around the door. With a wary half-smile, she said, "Sorry to disturb you. I know how much you were looking forward to clearing that lot today but I was downstairs, collecting my comb from the car, and overheard something interesting."

Sara set her pen down and gave Carla her full attention. "Go on."

"Apparently a woman is on her way to hospital after having her baby kidnapped."

Sara leapt to her feet and tore her jacket off the back of the chair. "You can fill me in on the way."

Carla smiled. "I thought you'd be interested."

"Interested wouldn't be my choice of word, try *concerned*."

"I stand corrected."

They made their way swiftly down the concrete staircase of Hereford police station, Sara's mind whirling with important questions that she was lining up to bombard Carla with once they reached the car. "We'll go in mine, I filled up on the way in this morning."

Once settled and Sara had pulled out into the heavy flow of traffic after a car had stopped to allow them out, she asked her first question. "Is the mother okay, or is that a super stupid question?"

"I'd plump for the latter. She's beside herself, they've had to sedate her. Mind you, if I were in her shoes, I'd be reacting exactly the same way, wouldn't you?"

"Indisputably. That poor woman. What about the husband?"

"Not sure. They couldn't get much out of her, she was talking gibberish and screaming for her baby when several members of the public found her. Someone called for the ambulance right away because they spotted blood. She couldn't tell them where it was from, but when the paramedics showed up, everything slotted into place. She'd been struck on the back of the head, which might also explain her talking nonsensically."

"Get you. I think I would be doing the same, wouldn't you?"

"Possibly."

"Have we got the names of the people who found her?"

"Yes. Fortunately, there were five people who stopped to assist her."

"Glad to hear it."

15

"Maybe she doesn't have a husband and is a single mum, have you considered that?"

"We won't know until we get there. And FYI, it wouldn't surprise me these days. Men rarely stick around once a woman has the baby... ouch, that was wrong of me to say that. Forget I uttered those words."

"Why? It's the truth. I bet the statistics will back us up, too. Most men want the fun and games of trying to get pregnant, but when the reality strikes, it all becomes overwhelming and at the first sign of a baby crying, they generally hit the road."

"Cynical but true, I suspect. Was there a pram found at the scene?"

"No, no sign of anything to do with a baby when uniform got there."

"How strange. This couldn't be a hoax, could it?"

Carla shrugged. "Who knows? I suspect we're about to find out."

After making the short trip and collecting a ticket at the barrier, Sara parked in the hospital car park and switched off the engine. "Another costly ticket coming my way. Let's get in and out of there sharpish, I'm struggling for cash this side of pay day."

"I can pay, don't worry."

They left the car and walked towards the main entrance.

"Sorry, I don't mean to moan, I don't usually complain. I've had a lot of expense this month, both insurances to find, car and house."

"You don't have to explain. Mine are spaced out throughout the year, thank goodness, I'd never cope otherwise. They're all healthy chunks out of our salaries these days, but then again, what isn't? Everything is going up at an alarming rate, and there's sod all we can bloody do about it."

"Yeah, don't get me started on that one. It's been a topic of conversation amongst my friends and family for months now. My sister is really struggling to keep her house going. I've advised her to downsize from her three-bedroom to a two, but she's having none of it."

"Has she thought about taking in a lodger?"

"Have you met my sister?" Sara laughed. "Lesley isn't the easiest person to live with."

"Needs must in times such as this."

"I'll drop the suggestion the next time I see her... and run, because she's liable to try and throttle me."

Carla grimaced. "For making a suggestion? Is she that volatile?"

"Believe me, she can be, when pushed."

They approached the reception desk and spoke to one of the two women on duty.

Sara flashed her ID. "We've had a call about a young woman being brought in, her baby may have been kidnapped. Sorry, I didn't catch her name."

"It's okay. I know the one you mean. Let me dig out the information for you. Ah, here it is, Eve Randall. You'll find her on the Women's Ward."

"Which is?"

"Second floor at the end of the corridor. The lift is behind you."

"Thanks, you'd think we should know that by now, the number of times we've had to come here over the past year."

The receptionist smiled, nodded and got back to work. They hopped on the lift and rode it up to the second floor in silence, Sara's mind racing, sorting out how to play this one. She drew a blank and soon realised she would need to gauge her approach once she'd spoken to the victim.

"Are you ready for this?" Sara asked.

Carla shrugged. "Not really. Is there an alternative on the table? Asking for a friend."

Sara smiled. "I wish. Let's see what she has to say and take it from there."

Sara produced her ID at the nurses' station, and a petite blonde nurse smiled.

"Ah, yes. Eve was in a bit of a state when she arrived. We've managed to calm her down, but that means she's been sedated."

"In other words, we're not likely to get much out of her, are we?"

"In truth, I'm not sure. The decision was made out of necessity. It was either that or allowing her to come in here, disrupting everyone. We couldn't have that."

"Don't you have any private rooms available for her?"

"Not at the moment, no. I assure you, she's better off on the ward, given the state she was in."

"I wasn't suggesting otherwise. I appreciate how difficult this situation must be for all of you. Can we see her now?"

"I'll introduce you to her rather than you show up at her bedside and start bombarding her with questions."

"One more question, if I may? Has she mentioned her husband at all?"

"Yes, we've contacted him. He's on his way down here now."

"Where was he?"

"Up in Newcastle. He's a travelling salesman, he sells blinds."

"Ah, I see. Thanks."

"No problem. If you'd care to join me." The nurse led them to Eve's bed. On the way, she shared some banter with a few of the patients. She poked her head through a gap in the curtain shielding Eve from the rest of the ward. "Hello, Eve, how are you feeling?"

"Okay, I guess. When can I leave? When is Paul getting here?"

"Paul is on his way. He shouldn't be too long. I've got some visitors for you. Two ladies from the police. Are you up to speaking with them?"

"Yes, yes, I want them to know what happened."

Sara listened to Eve's slurred responses from the other side of the curtain and didn't hold out much hope of getting much sense out of her when the interview began.

The nurse stepped aside and drew the curtain back enough for Sara and Carla to enter.

Sara showed the distraught woman her ID. "Hello, Eve. I'm Detective Inspector Sara Ramsey, and this is my partner, Detective Sergeant Carla Jameson. I'm sorry to hear what happened to you. Are you up to speaking with us?"

"I want my baby back. Why can't people understand that? You shouldn't be here questioning me, you should be out there, looking for her." Eve's head flopped back onto the pillow as if the air had been knocked out of her.

Sara took a step forward and sat in the chair next to Eve. She reached for the young woman's hand to comfort her, but Eve yanked it out of her grasp.

"I neither want nor need anyone's sympathy, all I want is my Mia back." Tears gushed, and her cheeks glistened under the strip light in no time at all. "My beautiful Mia, I need to hold her in my arms... to make me whole again. I'm nothing without her."

"I can totally understand that. You have my word that we will do everything in our power to find her. Unfortunately, I'm going to have to spend a few minutes with you first, trying to find out what happened, if you're up to telling us?"

"I wish I knew." Her gaze drifted to the curtain behind Sara. "I think I was on a call from my husband, or had I finished it? I can't be sure, everything is a bit hazy."

"Take your time, we'll work our way around it. Where were you?"

She paused for a moment or two. "I remember coming out of Aylestone Park and my phone ringing, yes, it was Paul. We chatted for a while as I walked. I was heading home, but as it was a nice day, I decided to take the scenic route, through the estate at the other end of the park. I wish I hadn't bothered now. Why did I go that way? Why?" Fresh tears splashed onto her pale cheeks.

Sara reached out a hand, but Eve withdrew hers and placed it over her chest, which Sara noticed was rising and falling erratically.

"Take your time. What happened next?"

"Paul rang, told me about his day. He asked me about the mother and baby group I had attended, and then we ended our conversation. I put my phone in my pocket, and then someone must have whacked me from behind. That's the last thing I remember. Why? Why would someone do that? Where have they taken Mia? I need her back, she's only six months old. She'll be going frantic. Every time I leave the room, she kicks up a fuss. How will she react without me being there? I need her. You have to find her, bring her back to me. I won't be able to live without her, knowing that someone has taken her and is probably raising her as their own." Eve heaved.

There was a bowl on the cabinet beside her. Sara leapt out of the chair and held it under Eve's chin. "Try not to upset yourself. I know that's easier said than done, we're going to do all we can to bring her home."

Eve emptied her stomach contents into the bowl. Sara retched inside but hid her true feelings in front of the desperate woman.

"I'm sorry. You don't want to see that, you're not a nurse, they're used to it. I've done nothing but vomit since they brought me in. I'm not usually the type."

"You've had a knock on the head, that's likely the cause. I

have a strong stomach, don't worry. Do you have any idea how long your husband is going to be?"

"A few hours yet. He's going to need to tie up a few things in Newcastle before he can get on the road."

A man whose baby has gone missing has chosen to stay and tie things up instead of rushing home to be with his wife? "I have to ask, have either you or your husband had any issues with any outsiders recently? Someone who might want to harm either of you perhaps?"

"No. We tend to keep ourselves to ourselves. We don't mix that often with people, that's why I found it difficult taking the plunge to join the mother and baby group. I put it off for weeks, but once I'd plucked up the courage to go, I found I really enjoyed it." She gasped and slapped a hand over her mouth. "You don't suppose one of them followed me and took the baby, do you?"

Sara tutted. "We won't know until we've questioned the people you met up with today. Where's the group based?"

Eve closed her eyes and swallowed. "It's on Folly Lane. I can't remember the name of it, sorry, my head is killing me."

"Try not to put extra stress on yourself. I'm sure we'll find it, there can't be too many M and B groups around there."

"Wait, I spoke to Becky, she's the co-owner, I think."

"There you go, that's a great help, thanks. How many people were there today, can you recall?"

"Gosh, now you're testing me. I think maybe around twenty mothers, probably three or four staff, including Becky."

"That's great. And you got on well with everyone?"

"Yes, I mostly hung out with a group of five other women during my time there. They're the only ones who stepped forward to involve me."

"Can you tell me their names?" Sara withdrew her notebook from her pocket.

Eve paused and rubbed her temple as if willing the names to come forward in her confused mind. "Let me see, there was Claudine, Francis, Gail and… I can't think of the other two ladies' names. Why can't I remember? I spent a couple of hours with them, you'd think I'd be able to bloody summon up their names."

"No pressure. Take your time."

"But we haven't got time, I need you to ask what you need to know and get out there. Every minute Mia is missing is taking her further and further away from me."

"I'm aware of that, but I promise you, the more information you can supply, the more likely we are to find her."

"My baby, I want her back. I feel so useless, lying here. My head is spinning. I can't even remember what she looks like, why can't I remember what colour eyes she has? I feel so inadequate."

"It's the medication. Try not to get too worked up about this, Eve. We're going to do our best to get Mia back. Is there anything else you can recall from your walk around the park? Did anyone speak to you?"

"A few couples when they walked past. I had taken a picnic with me. We sat on the benches at the top of the hill. Mia was gurgling away happily in her pram. Several couples just said hello as they passed us on the path. No one approached us as such, you know, to tell me how cute Mia was, not like other days up there."

"Did you see anyone lingering close by? Perhaps in the wooded area behind the benches?" Sara tried to picture the layout of the park she had visited herself several times in the past.

"No, I don't think so."

"Do you have any other family members in the area?"

"Yes, Amelia and Sandra, my sisters. The staff have rung Sandra, she should be here soon. I hate disturbing either of them, or Paul for that matter, but I need them. I can't cope with this all on my own."

"No one is expecting you to. I'm sure none of them will mind. What about your parents?"

"They're both gone. They moved to Spain a few years ago and someone broke into their villa and set fire to their home. They were asleep in their beds upstairs, there's no way they could have got out. I miss them every single day. I'm devastated they never got to meet their only grandchild." Tears bulged once more.

"I'm sorry for your loss. Hey, please try to think positively about Mia."

"I am, and yet it's so hard. All I can think about is the danger she is probably in. Someone took her from me with an evil intent, otherwise, why would they take her? Why? What goes through someone's mind like that... to take a young baby... if not to harm it?"

Sara found it hard to express what she was truly feeling about the situation. She couldn't keep repeating herself, telling Eve to remain positive. She glanced up at Carla for help, but her partner turned away, probably feeling as useless as she was.

"What about around the house, have you had any cause to be alarmed about anything lately?"

"No, I don't think so. You have to believe me, this has come out of the blue. If I'd had any sort of warning sign that something along these lines might be in the air then I would have remained more vigilant. Saying that, how do you combat being attacked from behind?"

"You can't. Therefore, you mustn't blame yourself."

The curtain was whisked back, and a young woman with long brown hair, tied back in a ponytail, entered the area. "My God, Eve, are you all right? You look dreadful, love."

Eve held out a hand, and the other woman, whom Sara suspected was Sandra, came closer to the bed.

Sara rose from her seat and introduced herself and Carla. "I'm DI Sara Ramsey, and this is my partner, DS Carla Jameson."

"The police? What are you doing here? I hope you've got the whole of the force out there searching for my niece. Shame on you if you haven't."

Sara offered the woman a reassuring smile. "We will have soon. We need to get some background information from Eve first before we instigate any kind of search for Mia."

"What are you waiting for? Get on with it."

"Sandra, calm down. They've only just arrived and have been asking me dozens of questions."

"Don't tell me to calm down, not when my dear niece is missing. Where is she, do you know?" Sandra's question was aimed at Sara.

"Not at this moment, no. Please, you need to give us a chance to get the investigation underway. We can't do that without sifting through the facts first."

Sandra crossed her arms and tapped her foot. "Don't let me stop you."

The nurse appeared. "I'm sorry, I'm going to need to ask you to keep the noise down. Actually, one of you should leave. Our policy of two to a bed still stands, even in cases like this."

Sara's gaze dropped on Carla. "Sergeant Jameson, would you mind?" she asked, sensing that Sandra would put her foot down and insist she remained with her sister.

"Not at all. I'll be out in the hallway."

Sara smiled, appreciating her partner's willingness to oblige.

Carla left, and Sandra moved closer to her sister and sat in the chair Sara had recently vacated.

"What happened, love?" Sandra asked her sister. "The nurse didn't tell me much when she rang me at work."

"Do you want me to go over things with your sister?" Sara asked Eve.

Eve nodded, winced and rested her head back against the pillow, utterly exhausted.

Sara ran through the events leading up to Mia's disappearance with the gobsmacked Sandra.

"My God, how could this have happened? And in broad daylight as well. What is this world coming to? Isn't anyone safe walking the streets during the day, let alone the night, around here nowadays?"

"We're doing our very best to ensure that happens, but resources are stretched to the max and getting worse yearly with every budget this government sets. But the last thing you want to hear from me is a bagful of excuses, as to why I perceive the criminals are making life more difficult for every copper working in this country during twenty twenty-three."

Sandra rolled her eyes and grunted. "Yeah, you can stick your excuses..."

"Sandra, be nice," Eve warned. "Piss her off, and where will that leave us, me? Better still, why don't you bugger off and let me deal with the investigating officer on my own?"

Sandra bounced to her feet. "Well, that's bloody gratitude for you. I leave work, concerned about your safety. Worried about my niece's well-being, only for you to frigging tell me to do one."

Eve closed her eyes and sighed. "I'm sorry. I know you mean well, but I need you to talk nicely to the main person who can help me find my daughter. That's not too much to ask, is it, sis?"

Sandra's shoulders slumped in either resignation or defeat, Sara wasn't quite sure which.

"I'm sorry. You're right, of course you are. When aren't you? You've always been the wisest one. Amelia and I are sadly lacking in that department. Please forgive me, Inspector."

"There's nothing to forgive. You have every right to question me for being here when I should be out there searching for Mia. Unfortunately, there are procedures we need to follow. Maybe you can fill in some blanks for me."

"I can try. What do you need to know?"

"If there has been anyone in Eve and Paul's life who might want to wish them harm."

Sandra gasped, and her head shot round to Eve. "No, is that what this is all about? Someone taking revenge? Have you come up against anyone who would do such a thing, love?"

"No, I couldn't think of anyone, but my head is so thick, either from the knock I received or from the medication they've given me. I'm struggling to think straight."

Sandra faced Sara once more. "Then my answer remains no. What sort of petty-minded people are walking the streets that they would think of snatching a baby after a falling-out with the parents?"

Sara raised an eyebrow. "You'd be surprised. What about ex-partners for both you and your husband?" she asked Eve.

"Gosh, now you're testing me," Eve said. She stared ahead of her, her brow wrinkling as she contemplated the question. "Paul and I have been together over ten years. Do you really think we should go back that far?"

"Can you recall any of your or your husband's exes making any threats in the past?"

"Not as far as I'm concerned. We all split up amicably enough. I never really went out with anyone for that long, maybe a few weeks, tops. I believe Paul said that the longest relationship he'd ever had was three days. That's how we knew we belonged together. We got married after six months and we'd been trying for a baby ever since. Mia came along just as we were considering looking at alternative methods of conceiving."

"I see. And you get on well with your neighbours?"

"Yes. The ones closest to us all seem friendly enough. We don't mix with them as such, we much prefer spending our spare time by ourselves or with our families. That's mostly during the summer, though."

"I can vouch for that," Sandra said. "Eve and Paul are very much a loved-up couple, we rarely get a look-in these days. I think it's been like that since we lost Mum and Dad."

The sisters clutched hands and fell silent.

Sara nodded. "I understand. Okay, I think we've got all we need for now. I'll be in touch if anything else crops up."

"Where do you begin searching for her?" Eve asked, her voice breaking on a sudden sob.

"We'll do the usual, check out any cameras in the area, but I'm also going to call an early press conference. I don't usually make that decision until we get further into a case. However, I feel it's essential to get the word out there. We'll also conduct house-to-house enquiries in the area where Mia was abducted. Maybe one of the neighbours either saw or heard something significant that will point us in the right direction and get the case underway."

"Good, I'm glad you're taking this seriously," Sandra muttered, her snarky tone in full flow once more.

"Don't worry, we'll definitely be taking this case very seriously indeed, you have my guarantee on that. I'm going to shoot off now. I'll leave you both one of my cards in case anything else comes to mind. Don't hesitate to get in touch, day or night."

"We won't," Eve replied. "Umm... would it be all right if

Paul contacts you when he gets here? He's bound to want to introduce himself to you."

"I'll look forward to hearing from him. I also want to leave you with these reassuring words: my team won't stop searching for Mia until we've found her, you have my word on that."

"Thank you. There's nothing left to say but to wish you good luck, Inspector. Please bring my baby home, she's all we've got. She'll be going frantic without us near her," Eve insisted.

Sara smiled. "I'll be in touch soon. Take care of yourself in the meantime, and listen to the doctors, you need your rest to recover from your injuries."

Eve waved her hand in front of her. "I'm fine. A small bump on the head is nothing compared to my daughter being abducted and in the hands of a monster for all we know."

Sara heard the anxiety rising in Eve's tone once more, her feelings ebbing and flowing, overwhelming her at times, which was to be expected in the circumstances.

Sara patted the back of Eve's hand. "The only advice I can offer you at this stage is to remain positive."

"I will, however, it's going to be difficult."

"You have Sandra and Amelia around to give you all the support you need."

"I'm lucky in that respect, and Paul, of course. I hope he shows up soon. I need him."

"It's a fair old distance for him to travel. I'm sure he's doing his best to get here quickly," Sara said unable to hide the sarcasm in her tone. In her opinion, he should have moved heaven and earth to be with her. She waved goodbye and drew back the curtain.

The nurses glanced up as she approached the desk.

"Thanks for letting me see her. Take care of her for me, I know she's in safe hands."

"She is, don't worry," the blonde nurse said. "Do you have any idea what happened to the baby?"

"No. We're about to begin our investigation in earnest now. We'll see what comes to light over the next few hours and days."

The two nurses held up their crossed fingers.

"Let's hope so," the blonde said. "I can't imagine how traumatic this must be for Eve, I'd be in bits. I think she's been very brave."

"Right, I'll leave you to it. Thanks again. Hopefully I'll be able to share some good news sooner rather than later."

"Good luck to you and your team, Inspector."

Sara smiled and left the ward. She found Carla scrolling through her mobile, leaning against the wall close to the entrance to the ward.

"Oh, hi. How did it go with the sister?"

"Let's walk and talk."

They upped their pace and headed towards the lift at the end of the corridor.

Once inside, Sara said, "Her sister finally calmed down after you left. Why do some people insist on shouting the odds at me when they don't even know me? Yeah, don't answer that, it was a rhetorical question that I usually keep to myself."

"Okay, I won't bother. What's our next step, bearing in mind we're up against it on this one?"

"If you do the driving, I can get the ball rolling. We need to arrange a press conference first and foremost but also need to get the team moving at the same time. I'll have a word with the desk sergeant when we get back, see how many uniformed officers he can supply."

"For house-to-house et cetera?"

"You've got it. We need every available officer working this case if we're going to save that vulnerable infant. Why would someone choose to attack a mother and snatch her baby?"

"I can name a number of scenarios that spring to mind."

"All right, let's have them. I have to admit I'm struggling to get a foothold on this one."

"Could be a woman, or man come to that, with mental health issues. Maybe they've recently lost a baby and found the whole scene of Eve pushing the baby around the park, sharing a picnic with her, just too much to handle. Or we might be looking at something far more sinister."

Sara closed her eyes and shook her head. "God, don't go there."

"We have to. People trafficking is on the rise, it was only a matter of time before they started going after the children."

"I know but I'd still rather not go down that route just yet."

"I think it would be foolish of us to dismiss it, even at this early stage."

"I have no intention of dismissing it, I'd rather simply deal with the facts and not think along such drastic lines right now."

She threw Carla the keys, paid for the parking at the huge meter outside the main entrance, and then jumped in the passenger seat. Carla drove up to the barrier, inserted the ticket, and then got on the road back to the station.

"Would it be worth checking with the hospital?" Carla asked before Sara could make her first call.

"About what specifically?"

"Ask the question, see if anyone has lost a baby lately."

Sara sighed. "I'm not sure. That could lead us into a dark and dreary place that I'm not sure I want to go, not yet."

"It's up to you, of course. I'm putting it out there as an alternative."

"Let's see how the initial investigation goes first, and we'll revisit the idea in a few days, how's that?"

"You're the boss."

Sara winced at her partner's abrupt tone but chose to ignore it and instead placed her first call to the press officer. "Hi, Jane, it's Sara Ramsey. I'm after an emergency press conference, can you oblige?"

"Hi, Sara. Sure. Tell me what you need and when."

"It's for a woman called Eve. Unfortunately, she was attacked a few hours ago, she's currently lying in a hospital bed."

"Poor woman, is she okay?"

"Far from it. Her six-month-old baby was abducted at the same time. She was knocked unconscious and is dealing with the consequences of receiving a bash to the back of the head."

"What the...? Oh my, how awful. Do you have any idea who took the baby?"

"No, that's why I need your help. There's nothing in either her or her husband's past that would indicate the attack and abduction was carried out by someone known to them at this stage."

"Crap, okay. Give me half an hour, no, make that fifteen minutes, and I'll get back to you."

"Hopefully with some good news."

"You can count on me, I haven't let you down yet, Sara."

"I know you haven't. Get back to me when you can. I have a number of phone calls to make, message me if you can't get through."

"I'll be sure to do that."

Sara ended the call and rang the incident room. Marissa answered the phone. "Hi, Marissa, it's me. We're on our way back, but I want to make sure we get the ball rolling ASAP on this one."

"Rightio, boss. What do you need from us?"

"First of all, I need Craig and Barry to work their usual magic on any CCTV footage they can find covering Aylestone Park. Then I need you and Jill to get on the road for me. Christine can cover the phones and do the necessary background checks."

"On the road?"

"Yes, we need to join in with the house-to-house enquiries to help uniform out. There's a baby's life at stake. I'm in the process of arranging a press conference now. The quicker we get the word out to the shit who abducted this baby, the sooner little Mia will be reunited with her mother and the rest of her family."

"I agree, boss. Jill and I will get out there right away. I think Craig has already sourced some of the footage from the area, you know what he's like, always jumping the gun."

"He's a good 'un. I thought as much. You set off. I'm going to have a word with the desk sergeant on my way in, see if he can give us any extra bodies. If he's up for it, I'll send them your way as soon as I can."

"No problem, boss. See you later, we'll get in touch if anything comes to light."

No sooner had Sara ended the call when her phone rang again and Jane's name lit up her tiny screen. "That was quick."

"Have I ever let you down in the past?"

"Nope, never. When do you need me?"

"Two o'clock suit you?"

Sara glanced at the clock on the dashboard which was reading one-forty. "I better get my arse into gear then. I'll meet you in the anteroom a couple of minutes beforehand."

"I'll be there. Is there anything else you need in the meantime?"

"I don't think so. I'll be in touch if I think of anything."

Sara ended the call, tipped her head back and puffed out her cheeks. "I hope I don't mess this up."

"What? You? Never. Why are you doubting yourself?"

Sara faced Carla and said quietly, "I think because of the responsibility this conference holds. We've got a six-month-old baby missing, for fuck's sake. Why? Who would do such a thing to a mother? How can anyone look after a child as well as its mother can?"

Carla grunted. "That's debatable at times from what I see daily round our way. You want to see how some of those parents treat their kids. The number of times I've overheard what some of the parents have said and have shot out of my chair, only for Des to restrain me and warn me not to get involved."

"Why have the sprogs in the first place if they don't know how to treat them with kindness and respect?"

"My thoughts exactly. Some of the parents need locking up, I can tell you. And I'm talking about the damn mothers here. Some of the fathers have already spent time inside, mostly on drug-related charges."

"Why live there? You can do so much better than that, Carla."

"Can I? On my salary, I don't think so."

"Wait a minute, doesn't Des stump up money for the rent as well?"

"Most of the time, yes, but sometimes he forgets to pay, and I find it a struggle asking him to dip his hand in his pocket."

"Jesus, I had no idea. Why didn't you tell me?"

"Why? Look at the way you're grinding your teeth now."

"Shit, sorry. It's only because I care about you. Want me to have a word with him?"

"Fucking hell, definitely not. I'm quite capable of fighting my own battles."

"Then do it. Don't let him get away with it. I have to say, I've never had a day since I met Mark where I've needed to ask him for cash for any of the bills."

"Well, good for you."

"Sorry, not what you wanted to hear. Ignore me. You don't have much luck with fellas at all, do you?"

Carla had previously been involved with a fireman who had turned out to be an abusive fucker behind closed doors. She'd eventually seen sense and given him the elbow only to hook up a few months later with Des who was an inspector over in Worcester. Once they'd become an item, he'd transferred to Hereford, and they had moved into a flat together.

"He's different from the other one, so don't start on at me about him. This is a blip that I need to find the confidence to change."

"Sounds like you have it all under control," Sara replied unconvincingly.

Carla indicated and pulled into the station car park. After she had reversed into Sara's designated space, they got out and entered the main entrance to find the desk sergeant, Jeff, talking to a couple of uniformed constables.

"All right if I have a quick word, Jeff?" Sara asked.

"You've had your break, get back to work now. Let me know how you get on later." He dismissed the two young men and then gave Sara his full attention. "All yours, ma'am."

"Jeff, I need to ask a huge favour. The assault that took place near Aylestone Park earlier."

He nodded, and a sadness overshadowed his features.

"I want to throw as many resources towards the task as possible."

"If you don't mind me saying, I would, too, ma'am, especially with the nipper going missing. Let me know what you need and I'll do what I can to lend a hand."

"A couple of my team members are on their way over there now to help the uniforms. Any chance you can supply more officers to cover the house-to-house enquiries in the area? The quicker we carry those out the better. I'm about to hold an urgent press conference, who knows what information is likely to come our way from that? I've never had to deal with a baby being kidnapped before."

"I can't say I have either. Whatever you need, give me a shout, and I'll get it sorted for you ASAP, ma'am."

"Thanks, Jeff, I knew I could count on you."

Sara smiled and punched her code in the security keypad. Upstairs, the rest of the team were hard at it. Not for the first time, she felt proud to be in charge of a group of people who cared about their work.

"How are you all getting on?"

"I'm going through the couple's finances now but haven't found anything strange lurking, boss," Christine was the first to respond.

Craig raised his hand and shrugged. "Same with the footage, there's little to none to be had, especially over that side of the park, in and around the estate. It's a different matter on the other side, near the car park, which is off the main road."

"I thought as much. Did you manage to spot the victim entering the main entrance?"

He tapped his keyboard and angled the screen towards her as she approached his desk. Carla set off to fetch them both a coffee and joined them a few moments later.

"Here she is, pushing the pram." Craig pointed at the screen.

Sara shook her head. "A picture of happiness. Look at the

glow on her face as she speaks to the baby. A far cry from what she looks like now, sitting up in hospital, doped up to the eyeballs to keep her calm."

Craig whizzed the disc along a few minutes until they saw Eve pushing the pram around the winding path, making her way up to the top of the hill.

Sara sipped at her coffee. "We can only just make her out. We wouldn't be able to tell who she was if we hadn't clocked her at the entrance. What I'm getting at is, she mentioned she spoke to a few couples while she ate her lunch. We're not going to be able to get a good view of them from this angle."

"I can follow them as they wind their way around the park, providing they come back to the main entrance, boss. However, if they decide to go the other way then we're waist-high up the proverbial creek."

"Do your best for me, Craig, it's all we can do at the moment. I've only got a few minutes before I'm needed downstairs. I'll be in my office, making some notes. Keep up the good work, folks. Do what you can this side of the conference. Hopefully, once it has been aired, we'll be inundated with calls."

"You have high hopes there," Carla muttered.

"Yeah, it might be wishful thinking on my part, but if we don't have positive thoughts about this case, I might as well hang up my cuffs for good now." She picked up her coffee and swept into the office, ignoring the usual view of the Brecon Beacons and moving directly to her desk where she scribbled down a couple of pages of notes, her coffee going cold in the process.

Carla knocked on the door and stuck her head around it ten minutes later. "I know how you get caught up in things. I wanted you to be aware of the time, that's all."

"Thanks, partner. I'm on my way down there now. Keep on top of things around here in my absence."

Carla cocked an eyebrow. "I won't need to, they're all hard at it as usual. Anything specific you want me to do?"

"Yes, look up the mother and baby group, see until what time they're open, and we'll drop by to see them once I'm done being grilled by the journalists."

"We should try and fit in some lunch as well. Not that I spend most of my time thinking about food or anything."

"Okay, we'll drop into the baker's on our way out. Not sure I'm up to eating anything, my stomach is in knots at the thought of appearing in front of the cameras."

"You'll be fine. You're heaping too much pressure on your shoulders. You're going to have to reassess how you treat this case."

"It's going to be difficult. I've never had such a young life at stake before. It's hard to know what to do for the best."

Carla tutted. "In my eyes, you shouldn't be treating this investigation any different from the dozens of other cases we've dealt with over the years."

Sara smiled and nodded. "I wish you'd tell my heart and mind that." She rose from her chair and shook her arms out. "There, all better now."

"Yeah, right. Come on, Sara, you've got this. Deep down, you know that's true."

"Do I? I'm glad you have faith in me."

"I do, an immeasurable amount of faith, and if I have to, I'll kick you up the backside a few times until you start believing in yourself once more."

"There's no need to go that far, I promise." Sara gathered her notebook and pen from the desk and followed Carla out of the office. "Wish me luck, guys. Let's hope the conference paves the way for us finding the baby, and quickly."

Carla rubbed Sara's upper arm and winked. "We all have faith in you."

"Thanks." Sara turned and raced out of the incident room

and down the stairs to the awaiting pack of journalists, unsure what to expect from them on this one.

Jane welcomed her with a cheery smile and comforting words. "Don't look so worried, you should be used to this lot by now."

"It's not them I'm worried about... well, I suppose it is, really."

"I know what you're going to say next. The fact that you're dealing with a tiny baby is what's unnerving you, am I right?"

"One hundred percent right. Carla said I've got to treat it just like any other case we deal with. Sorry, but I'm struggling to get my head around that, to the point that I'm considering handing the case over to someone else."

Jane's mouth gaped open for a second or two. "Are you kidding me?"

Sara thumped her thighs for airing her thoughts. "Sorry, I shouldn't have said anything. I'm not even sure if that's how I feel or not. I'm finding this whole case very confusing and I've only been on it a few hours. Maybe I should have swerved it from the get-go."

"Nonsense. Hey, if my child went missing, I know your name would be at the top of my list for the lead investigator."

"You sure know how to make a girl feel wanted."

"Nothing of the sort. It happens to be the truth, Sara. I've worked with dozens of DIs and DCIs over the years, and I have to say, whenever you get in touch needing me to organise a conference for you, my heart flutters. Oh gosh, that sounds gushy. What I'm trying to say is, never doubt yourself, you're one hell of an investigator. Hey, don't take my word for it, after we're done here, you need to return to your office and go through your statistics going back over the last few years and see what you've achieved."

Sara held her hands up in submission. "All right, consider

myself told. We'd better crack on. Have many shown up today?"

"Not sure if I should tell you this or not, but we've got a full house in there."

"Shit, yeah, maybe you should have kept that one to yourself, for now."

Jane chuckled. "You'll be fine, you always are. You're a natural on the stage, and if you falter, I'll be there, right beside you to prompt you."

"Thanks, Jane. Let's get on with it before nerves get the better of me and leave me tongue-tied."

Jane led the way out of the anteroom. As the door opened, Sara kept her focus on the stage that Jane had set up, instead of taking in the audience ahead of her. That changed once she was sitting on the stage and the cameras started rolling. With her heart pounding, she relayed all the information she intended to share with the journalists. Unbelievably, they let her make her plea without their usual interruptions and, scanning the room, Sara noticed a few eyes glistening with tears under the unforgiving strip lights, which pleased her. It conveyed that the journalists were about to take this case far more seriously than any of the others she had ever put before them.

They listened intently and quietly until Sara had completed her announcement, then a few hands rose, if a little tentatively.

"Is the mother okay?" a female journalist asked from the front row.

"She's devastated and in hospital at present, nursing a bad injury to her head."

"Do you have any leads as yet, Inspector?" a male asked, sitting alongside the female.

"Not yet. My team are out there, conducting house-to-house enquiries of the area, and we are carrying out further checks with the information and technology at our disposal."

"But clues are lacking, I take it, otherwise you wouldn't be calling this press conference so early into the investigation, would you?" another gentleman said from the back of the room.

"I felt the need warranted calling an early press conference. I thought it was imperative to reach out to the person who has taken baby Mia, in the hope that they might reconsider their actions and come forward with the child." Sara stared down the camera to make a personal plea to the kidnapper. "Please, if you're the one who took the baby, her mother, Eve, is desperate to be reunited with her daughter. This is a vital stage in the child's development. Breaking the bond between mother and daughter at this time could have a detrimental effect on baby Mia. She needs her mother. Do the right thing and give her back. You can make a confidential call to the number at the bottom of your screen. No further action will be taken if you do the right thing for both the baby and her mother. Please, I'm begging you, if you need help, come forward, and we can get you all the help you need. Just return Mia to her mother who is lying in hospital, devastated and at her wits' end. Imagine being in her shoes. The feeling of uselessness and being overwhelmed by your inability to cuddle your child. Do the right thing and come forward. Eve needs to know her baby is safe. Reach out to us, and we'll do our utmost to ensure you get the help you need to get on with the rest of your life."

"Have you interviewed the mother, Inspector?" the older journalist at the back asked. "Like so many cases of this ilk, it's usually someone from the parents' past that is the instigator behind the abduction. Could that be the case this time?"

"Yes, I've interviewed the mother. To be truthful, the

doctor had decided to sedate her to ease the stress she's under. During the interview, she couldn't give me a single reason why someone she knew would take the baby. I'm pleading with the public to come forward with any information they might have. For instance, has a family member or friend suddenly shown up with a baby they didn't have last week? We can't do this without the help of the general public. We have a population of just over one hundred and ninety-three thousand in this city. Someone, somewhere, must know something. Please, please get in touch. It doesn't matter if it doesn't sit right with you, we're talking about an innocent baby's life being at stake here. Think of the baby, let's put the baby first in all of this."

"And if no one comes forward with any useful information?" a woman at the end of the front row asked. "What's your next step, Inspector?"

"I can't divulge that at this stage," Sara tried to bluff her way out of the situation.

"In other words, you haven't thought that far ahead yet?"

"We have procedures in place for every conceivable situation you can think of, I assure you. My team and I will be following those procedures to the letter."

"What about resources on this one, Inspector?" another journalist in the front asked.

"We'll be throwing all the resources we can muster that are at our disposal. No stone will be unturned in our search for little Mia. But we're still going to be reliant on the public's help. Don't let us down. Call the number today if you can help. Even if there is something not sitting right with you about a neighbour who has suddenly turned up with a baby. Don't hesitate to get in touch with us. But we need your calls today, at your earliest convenience, if we're going to reunite Mia with her mother."

"Any more questions for the inspector?" Jane asked the audience.

When the room fell silent, she closed the press conference, thanking all those who had attended, then she and Sara left the stage and returned to the anteroom.

"There, it was a breeze for you. All that unnecessary worrying. You were the utter professional out there, like you always are."

"Thanks. I'd be super crap at this if I didn't have you sitting up there alongside me, Jane. When will the conference be aired?"

"During the afternoon via the radio and on the early evening news via the TV. I hope it reaps you the rewards you need to solve this investigation, Sara."

"Me, too. Thanks again for setting all this up so swiftly, Jane."

They hugged and set off in different directions.

Sara trudged her way back up the stairs, suddenly feeling drained. It had been a long day, physically and emotionally, and there were still several hours ahead of her, if not more.

"How's it all going?" she asked the team after entering the room.

"We're plodding on. How did the conference go?" Christine said.

Before Sara could answer, the phone on Christine's desk rang.

She answered it and looked directly at Sara. "Just a moment, I'll let DI Ramsey know."

Sara tilted her head to one side. "Let me know what?"

"That the husband is downstairs, demanding to see you."

Sara tipped back her head and groaned. "Can this day get any better? Okay, tell Jeff I'll be down in five minutes. Can you ask him to put Paul Randall in an interview room and offer him a drink in the meantime?"

"Will do, boss."

"Shit, that's all I need. I thought he'd go straight to the hospital to be with his wife."

"Maybe he went there first," Carla suggested. "Want me to come down there with you?"

"Yeah, I think that would be a great idea. Thanks, partner. I'm just going to run a comb through my hair, something I neglected to do before the conference."

Carla laughed. "You worry too much about your appearance. By that I mean, that you always look the part, you never let the Force down."

"Thanks, I'm not sure I believe you half the time. I'll be back in a second."

"I'll meet you in the hallway."

Sara nipped into the office and attacked her hair with her comb, pulling out a few knots that had developed during the day, then she left the room and popped to the loo. She found Carla leaning against the wall in the hallway by the notice-board, scrolling through her phone as usual.

Sara reappeared a few minutes later, her bladder empty, ready to tackle what lay ahead of her.

After making her way downstairs, she poked her head into the reception area. "What room is he in, Jeff?"

"Room One, ma'am. I've given him a coffee. Be warned, he's not in the best of moods."

"To be expected in the circumstances. Thanks for the heads-up."

"Don't take any shit from him, Sara, our job is hard enough as it is without people marching in here and tearing us apart when we're doing our very best for them."

"To be fair, he doesn't know that, not yet. Let's cut him some slack for now, eh?"

"If you say so."

Sara entered Interview Room One and introduced Carla

and herself to a tall man leaning against the back wall. His suit was well cut, and his tie loosened at the neck told Sara all she needed to know about him. His hair was tousled as if he'd been constantly running his hands through it on the drive down from Newcastle. "Hello, Mr Randall, is it all right if I call you Paul?"

"If you like."

"I'm pleased to meet you. I'm DI Sara Ramsey, and this is my partner, DS Carla Jameson. Shall we take a seat?"

"Why not? What news do you have for me? Wait, first of all, can you tell me why you're hanging around the station and not out there, searching for Mia?"

"In our defence, we've not long finished speaking to a room full of journalists. I felt there was a need to get the word out there quickly with this case, not something I usually entertain until we're a few days into the investigation and clues are thin on the ground."

"I see. And what do you hope to gain from putting out a conference at this time?"

The three of them sat at the table, and Paul sipped at his drink.

"I must admit that I took a gamble. Hopefully a member of the public will get in touch, informing us they've seen a neighbour with a child who has suddenly appeared."

"And the likelihood of that neighbour seeing the conference on the news is...?"

"Greater than if we hadn't bothered to put one out there. You're going to have to trust me on this one. Running a press conference can be an important way of highlighting the issue with the general public."

"You mean so the same thing doesn't happen to someone else's child?"

"That as well. Like I've already stated, it can put doubt in a person's mind and prompt them into getting in touch with us."

"Whatever. What are you *actively* doing to find my daughter?"

"Actually, quite a lot. As well as putting out an urgent press conference, we're also carrying out rigorous house-to-house enquiries in the area where Mia went missing."

"Is that it? What about alerting all the cars in the area to be on the lookout for a psychotic person pushing Mia's pram?"

"That goes without saying. An alert was issued immediately. The problem we're dealing with is that we don't know if your baby was taken by a male or female. Or even how they escaped the area. On foot, pushing the pram? Or did they bundle Mia and the pram into a car? We're hoping the conference and my team out, knocking on doors, will come up with the answers soon. Until such a time, our hands are tied."

He opened his mouth to speak, and Sara raised a finger and wagged it.

"I'm sorry if that's not what you want to hear at this time, but you need to know that we're doing our best to bring Mia home. How's your wife?"

He paused and chewed on his lip. "I don't know. No, that's a lie, I rang the hospital on the drive down, and they advised me to let her rest as she'd only just dropped off to sleep. They told me to go home, get some sleep and call back this evening. I'm going out of my mind with worry, and they virtually told me to steer clear of my wife, can you believe that? So, rather than pace the floor at home, surrounded by my beautiful daughter's toys, I thought I would come down here and meet the team in charge of our case."

"I can understand that. You must be tired after your long journey. Why don't you stay at a local hotel for the night?"

"I might do that later. For now, you're stuck with me, Inspector."

"Ah, well, the more time I spend around here talking to you the less time I can be with my team, organising what needs to be actioned, as and when things crop up. I'm sure you'll agree, that wouldn't be in either of our interest, would it now?"

"Okay, you've got me on that one. But I need to feel involved, all the same. You would, too, if the tables were turned. All I'm asking is for you to keep me in the loop and up to date on what's going on during the investigation."

"I promise you, as soon as anything significant rears its head, you'll be the first to know."

His eyes narrowed and he cocked his head. "One thing you should know from the outset, Inspector, I'm nobody's fool, so please never regard me as one."

"I'm glad to hear it, and just so we're clear, neither am I. I'll keep you informed to the best of my ability, however, my priority will always remain with your daughter, I need you to be aware of that fact. From experience, I realise there are going to be days when I won't have time to take an extra breath, let alone ring you with the details of what has happened. I'm sure you'll understand and appreciate my need to put your daughter's well-being before your own if such a time crops up, which I'm sure it will, during the course of the investigation."

"Okay, you've got me over a barrel there. I know how these things work, all I'm asking is that you don't forget about Eve and me throughout the case. You hear so many scare stories about how the police could, or should, have done better, that's all I'm trying to do here, prevent that from happening."

"You've made yourself perfectly clear, Mr Randall. I hope what I've had to say in return has put your mind at rest, if only a little. My team and I have an exemplary record that we're keen to keep intact throughout this investigation. All I'm asking is that you give us a chance."

He sat back, crossed his arms and smiled at her. "I like you, Inspector. I get the impression that you tell things as they are."

"That's very astute of you. As I've stated already, you have a crack team working the case, you have my word that we won't stop until we've found Mia."

"Thank you, that's what I was hoping to hear. I'm sorry for coming down here and shouting the odds, it's how I deal with people, to get the reaction I need from them."

"That might be successful in your working life, but for the record, it won't get you very far when dealing with the police. I might go as far as to say, had someone else been in charge of your daughter's case, you could have pissed the SIO off enough for them to want to unload the case files. That, again in my experience, would have only proved detrimental to the investigation. So I'm glad we've sorted things out at an early stage. Are you up to answering some questions while you're here, Mr Randall?"

A smile forced his lips apart. "But of course, Inspector. Feel free to ask me anything you like, within reason."

Sara's stomach churned at the way his tone had altered. *What's your game, Paul Randall?* She combatted the uneasy feeling seeping through her by smiling at him. "Can you think of anyone who might consider taking Mia? Or who would intentionally set out to hurt your wife?" She knew it was wrong of her to speculate, but there was something about this man that wasn't ringing true. *Is he having an affair? Has he had one in the past and it's come back to bite him in the arse? Is that why Mia has been kidnapped?*

"I can't, no. I've not fallen out with anyone lately. Thankfully, I don't have anyone that depraved sitting on my friends' list. Therefore, I'm at a loss to offer you any names. Believe me, I would if I thought it would lead you to my daughter, you have no worries on that front. I'm as much in the dark about who could do this as my wife probably was, if you got around to asking her the same question."

"I did. I also put the same question to your sister-in-law, Sandra, when she showed up at the hospital."

"Great, that's one person you shouldn't have asked."

Sara inclined her head. "May I ask why?"

"She's a gossip, pure and simple. She also has a vicious tongue in her head. Eve is always falling out with her."

"If that's correct, then why was she the first person Eve called to be with her at the hospital with you being so far away at the time?"

"Because her other sister, Amelia, is out of it most days, drugged up to the eyeballs on medication the doctor has supplied and probably a handful of others that she's bought online."

"I see. Am I to understand that you have a hard time dealing with Eve's sisters?"

"No, not at all. I tolerate them for her sake. The family grew closer together once Eve's parents died in that godawful fire. I refused to stand in the way of their grief, and to be honest with you, I expected things to return to normal once the funerals had been held. They didn't. Both sisters became very clingy, to the point of me feeling suffocated in my own home."

"That's why you prefer to be on the road?"

"Yes, the farther away the better most days once Sandra and Amelia started sticking their oar into our marriage. I thought everything would settle down once Mia was born; if anything, they got a hundred times worse. So, when my area manager told me they were struggling to plug the gap up in Newcastle and would I mind covering the area, I jumped at the chance. Don't get me wrong, while I love the bones of my wife and my daughter, it's the excess baggage I can't abide."

"Excess baggage being Sandra and Amelia, is that what you mean?"

Paul glanced down at his clenched hands. "It's the interference I can't stand. I married Eve, not her damn family. When her parents were alive, they kept their distance until we reached out to them for help. The same can't be said for the sisters. Especially Sandra who is a bit of a know-it-all who actually knows fuck all at the end of the day. Excuse my language."

"If they wind you up that much, have you tried having it out with them?"

"Believe me, I've tried, but Eve always holds me back. She's of the opinion that their parents' deaths have brought the girls closer together."

"And by the sounds of it you feel cast aside, am I right?"

He squeezed his hands together and wrung them. "Perhaps, I've never really thought about it like that."

"Do you think either of your sisters-in-law could be behind Mia's disappearance?"

"He studied his moving hands for a while longer then splayed them flat on the desk. "No, I don't think so. There again, who can tell nowadays? Amelia is off her head with medication most of the time. Have you had the pleasure of meeting her yet?"

"No, not yet. If you can give us her address, we'll call round and see her later today."

"It's flat five, Longlarton Road over in Belmont."

"I think I know the area. I take it she's there all the time, is she?"

"That's right. You'll find her vegged out in front of the TV most days, dosed up to the eyeballs."

"Does she have a partner? Boyfriend or husband?"

He laughed. "You really think anyone would put up with that kind of behaviour?"

"I see. I suppose it must have been hard for her losing her parents in that way. Grief affects people differently."

"If you say so. My parents always drilled it into me to hold my head up high and take what life has to offer on the chin."

That would explain your lack of emotion where your daughter is concerned then.

"Sounds like you had a very strict upbringing."

"My father was a major in the British army. We travelled the world, moved to a different country every few years. My brother and I had to grow up quickly or suffer the consequences."

"Those being?" Sara asked, intrigued.

"If we didn't obey or respect him, he would beat the crap out of us."

"Really? And the army put up with that?"

He laughed. "What happened took place behind closed doors. My mother was abused by my father every day of her life, but he made sure he never struck her where the bruises would show. We heard the screams, though, every day and night. Every time he was at home. The relief was evident in the house when he was away on duty. Mum was a totally different person."

"That must have been a tough life for you and your brother."

"It was, but it also made us value our lives more once we left home and started out on our own. Don't get me wrong, I love my parents and appreciate all they did for me when I was growing up, but my life as it stands now is far removed from what my father had planned out for me."

"Being a salesman?"

He nodded.

"Are your parents still alive?"

"Mum is, but Dad had a heart attack when he was in his fifties. He was beating Mum up at the time. God must have struck him down, it was about time. I was perceived to be a failure in his eyes."

"Why?"

"Because I didn't join the army like he did in his late teens. It was all he knew. He was good at his job, but the army life wasn't for me."

"What does your brother do for a living?"

He rolled his eyes and laughed a second time. "He joined the navy just to spite my father. You can imagine how well that went down at home."

"I can. And your mother? Where is she now?"

"She's down in Cornwall, living the dream. She was drawn to a little cottage down by the sea and lives a very peaceful existence."

"Do you see her much?"

"She comes to visit now and again but she's always itching to get back down there. I don't stand in her way, her happiness means everything to me. Witnessing the way her spirit was set free after Dad passed away was a revelation for all of us. I swore then that I would bend over backwards, do what was necessary, to give my wife and child everything they need, and now this..." His voice caught on the emotion welling up.

Sara reached across the table and placed her hand on his. "It's all right to show that you care about your family, you know."

He dragged his hand away and glanced at her. "Is it? Sometimes people believe it to be a weakness in men."

"Nonsense. My husband is a prime example, he's always wearing his heart on his sleeve, and furthermore, he's not ashamed to show it. Maybe this has more to do with the way you were brought up, by your father in particular, than you realise. To believe it's a form of weakness doesn't make sense to me. You're concerned, worried, terrified even that your baby has been taken. Sitting here rigid with an air of... what shall I call it? An air of indifference is only going to show you in a poor light."

He stared at Sara and shook his head. "I'm sorry, you're right. I'm guilty of pretending I'm a hard nut to crack when inside I'm a blithering mess. I feel helpless, not knowing where my baby is. All I keep wondering is if the person that has her is... abusing her, you know, physically. There are so many warped fuckers walking the streets these days." A tear slipped onto his cheek, and he swiped it away with the cuff of his jacket. "I swore I wouldn't do this. Crying is always a sign of weakness, my father bashed that into me in my teens. He'd know what to do, if he were still alive," he said out of the blue, shocking Sara.

"Your father? And what do you think he would do or say?"

"He'd be out there, forming a search party of his own. He wouldn't need the police to do his dirty work for him. And in the likelihood of him finding this person, he'd dish out his own punishment." He pointed at Sara and whispered, "And they wouldn't be able to walk away from him. Male or female, he wouldn't care, he'd break every frigging bone in their body and leave them clinging on for life."

Sara smiled. "In that case, I'm glad he's not here as he'd only make our job a whole lot harder, and I fear it's going to be hard enough as it is. You're going to have to trust us, believe in us. We're going to have to sit back for now and count on the general public to help us. Are you willing to give it a shot?"

He shrugged. "I don't think I've got a lot of choice, do

you? How many cases like this have you got under your belt, Inspector? Or shouldn't I ask?"

"I'm not going to lie to you, I've always maintained that honesty is the best policy. This is the first case I've dealt with where a child has been abducted. However, I want to assure you that I won't be treating this case any differently, and my team and I have a ninety-five percent success rate. Don't ask what happened to the other five percent, we don't mention that. Those cases were a long time ago, when we were finding our feet as a team."

"Sounds good enough to me. I trust you, Inspector. Don't let me down."

"I won't intentionally, I promise. I'm going to need you and your family to work with me, not against me if we're going to bring Mia home."

"That goes without saying."

"Can I ask why you felt the need to finish things off at work rather than come straight home?"

"I felt the need to stay up there, it was important at the time. Whether that was right or wrong, only time will tell."

"Fair enough, if that's what you believe. Now, if there's nothing else you can think of to tell me, I'm going to need to get on with the investigation."

"There isn't. There are no skeletons in my closet or anything else like that, I promise." He scraped his chair back and stood. "Do you need my number?"

"Yes, we'll swap numbers, that way you can keep in touch with me, if you need to. I'll get a Family Liaison Officer assigned to you."

"I won't pester you. I know that some parents in my position would feel the need to keep on top of you, but I'm sure you could do without the added stress, am I right?"

"You are. Furthermore, I appreciate you allowing us to get on with the investigation. I'm going to ensure that we don't let you down. I'll just need a recent photo of the baby, if you have one."

He selected a photo from his phone and she gave him her number to send it to. Then, while Sara walked ahead of Paul, Carla brought up the rear as they made their way back to the reception area. Sara went the extra mile and showed Paul to his car and shook his hand. "Take care of yourself and your wife. I'll be in touch as soon as I hear anything."

"I believe you. Thank you for putting up with my mood swings back there."

Sara smiled. "You're entitled to be emotional. Now go home or go to a hotel and get some rest."

He slipped into his car and she watched him drive away and turn left into the traffic that was already building on the main road, her stress levels lowering with his departure.

Sara glanced at her watch. "Shit, it's three already." She turned and tore through the main door and caught up with Carla in the incident room.

"Are you all right, did he give you any grief outside?" Carla asked, her brow wrinkled with confusion.

"No, he was fine. However, I've just noticed the time. I wanted to drop by and have a chat with the owner of the mother and baby group."

"Ah, it's all in hand. I took the liberty of ringing her. The call diverted to her mobile as the premises are shut now. I've got her address, she told me she'll be in for the next thirty minutes, if you want to pop out and see her."

Smiling, Sara said, "What are we waiting for then?" She spun around and spoke to the rest of the team before they left. "Any other news from anyone?"

Craig was the first to shake his head. "Disappointingly, nothing from us, boss, not yet."

"Okay, keep going, peeps. If anything, and I mean the slightest nugget of information surfaces, then get in touch

ASAP. Carla and I will get on the road. We're going to speak to the owner of the M and B facility and then drop by and have a word with Eve's other sister, see what she has to say."

TEN MINUTES LATER, Sara drew up outside a detached house not far from Aylestone Park. Becky Silva opened the door the second she saw them pull into the driveway.

"You must be Inspector Ramsey," she said. "I've not long heard you speaking on the news. I'm shocked and appalled by what I've heard. How's Eve? Can you tell me?"

"She's as well as can be expected in the circumstances. Shall we talk inside?" Sara glanced around her at the other houses in the immediate vicinity.

"Of course, do come in. I was about to make a drink, would you like one?"

"Thanks. Two white coffees would be great."

"Come inside. The kitchen is out the back. It's in a mess, though, I was in the middle of prepping the veg for dinner."

"Don't worry, I'm sure we've been subjected to a lot worse sights over the years. Have you owned the group long?"

"A couple of years. My partner, Gaynor, and I started it up once our own kids were old enough to attend secondary school. We've been delighted by its success. It's growing weekly now that word has got around. I'm in the middle of holding interviews for extra staff, have been for the past few days."

"How is that going?"

She invited them to sit at the oak table in the kitchen while she prepared the coffees. Becky held out her hand and waved it from side to side. "Lots of candidates, but they're not what I would call quality applicants, so I'm afraid our search continues."

"It must be difficult finding such a trustworthy applicant

to fill the post. I take it you carry out stringent background checks before you employ someone?"

"Yes, I'm super thorough. I have to be. Although the mothers are mostly with the babies at our place, we still need to ensure everything runs smoothly. There are times when a mother will leave her baby with us for an hour or two. I wouldn't be able to forgive myself if anything happened to someone's child in their absence."

Becky finished making the drinks and delivered them to the table. She placed a cup on the coaster in front of Sara and then Carla.

"Do you know Eve Randall well?"

Becky sat with a thump. "Not really. I spent a little while speaking with her this morning, reassuring her, if you like. This was her second visit to the group. She seemed very nervous when she joined us this morning but overall was less anxious when she departed. Can you tell me what actually happened? She told me she was going to the park to have a picnic with Mia."

"She successfully ate her lunch then left the park at the rear, went through the estate there. She received a call from her husband, and when she ended the call, someone bashed her on the back of the head. She's in hospital now, nursing a bad injury, possibly concussion."

"Oh my, that poor woman. And the person who attacked her then stole little Mia?"

"That's right. We don't know the ins and outs. My team are conducting enquiries in the area to see if anyone either saw or heard anything out of the ordinary around the time Eve was attacked. Hopefully, once the conference has been aired properly on the TV later, we'll start receiving positive feedback that we can act upon. Until such a time, it's a bit of a waiting game."

"In broad daylight, though. How often does that type of thing happen?"

"It's the first case we've come across. I believe the person who took Mia had it all planned out. The likelihood of being caught on camera in the area is out of the question."

"Oh my, how will you find Mia then, with no clues to go on? It's unthinkable to believe that someone could attack a mother pushing a pram in the street, with the intention of snatching her baby. My heart goes out to Eve, and her husband, of course."

"I hate to ask this, knowing how rigorously you vet your staff, but did you see or hear anything suspicious going on at the club this morning?"

"No, nothing at all. I would have told you the instant I saw you or rung the station if anything had come to mind during the appeal that went out on the radio. I'm in utter shock to think that someone has taken Mia, for what reason?"

"We're at a loss to know that with no clues to follow up. Would you say that Eve was accepted by all of the mothers at the group today?"

"Yes, it's a very friendly environment, it's what I strive for. Mothers need to know they feel safe. I don't think our business would be growing to the extent it has over the past couple of years if people didn't feel comfortable, do you?"

"Fair comment. Did you happen to see anyone lingering outside the property today at any time?"

"Gosh, now you're asking. Not that I noticed, nothing that really stood out to me, not that I was looking for anything along those lines. Who knew that taking your baby out for a picnic could end this way? I'm trying to put myself in Eve's shoes and I'm struggling. I think I would be going out of my mind with worry."

"The injury she sustained will be playing a major part in

how she'll probably be processing what's happened. We've not long interviewed her husband, and he told me the nurses have asked him to stay away so that she can grab some sleep. The doctor had sedated her when we visited her earlier."

"Just as well. I would need medication on drip if that was my baby someone had taken. You have to ask what goes through a person's mind when they sink that low."

"This is it, we don't know what we're dealing with right now. Have no idea what their motive is, everything is such a mystery to us at this time."

"It beggars belief. Do you think someone might have lost their own baby and set out to intentionally steal someone else's... Eve's?"

Sara shrugged. "We're doing the necessary checks on that at the moment."

"You have a tough job on your hands, I don't envy you, Inspector. If there is anything I can do for you, you only have to ask."

"Do you have cameras at the property?"

"Only overlooking the car park. You're welcome to view the footage from today when I open up tomorrow. No, you'll have enough on your plate as it stands. Why don't I make a copy of the disc and drop it over to the station in the afternoon, after I close up for the day?"

"That would be fantastic, thanks."

"It's the least I can do and will help keep me from drowning in helplessness. I still can't get my head around someone doing this. What that child must be going through, being cut off from her mother like that. It doesn't bear thinking about. She'll be going frantic when a stranger's face is staring down at her instead of her own mother's."

"I can imagine. Perhaps you can tell me if anyone has left the group under a cloud recently?"

"No, nothing is coming to mind. The only time people

leave is when their finances take a major hit, such as their marriage has ended or their partner has lost their job and they can no longer afford the fees. I would always bend over backwards for people if their circumstances change, and everyone knows they can always reach out to us."

"Then I think we're done here." Sara sipped at her lukewarm drink and stood.

"I can understand your need to want to get on with things. I'll sort out the disc and bring it over tomorrow, probably be around this time."

"Excellent news. Thanks for the drink and for chatting with us. Sorry to have to run off like this, we need to visit a few other people before the day is out."

"Of course you do. You don't owe me an apology, Inspector, you know what's best."

Becky showed them to the door, her shoulders slumped in despair and sadness. "Ring me if you need anything. I want to help the family as much as I can."

"I will. Take care of yourself. It was nice meeting you."

"You, too. I hope you find Mia soon. I can't bear to think of her being away from her mother for days on end."

"Hopefully, it won't come to that."

Sara and Carla walked back to the car and got in.

Sara let out an enormous sigh and hit her thigh. "Why is nothing going well for us on this one, why?"

"There you go again, being too harsh on yourself."

"I know but…"

"No buts. We can only do what we can, given the information we have to hand, which you know as well as I do, is minimal at this stage. There's no point in you letting your head drop, not now, nor in the future. We'll get Mia back. When? Well, that's hard to say. What I do know is that it's imperative to keep our spirits up and not let this case, or the fact that very few clues are coming our way, overwhelm us. You hear me?"

Sara nodded and started the engine. "I know you're talking sense, for a change, but it's still hard to deal with."

"It's early days. Give yourself, and us, a break, Sara. You're guilty of heaping too much pressure on yourself. You need to take a step back and start regarding this case like any other that comes our way. I've never seen you in such a state before."

"I know I'm letting it get to me, but we've never had to deal with… no, I'm not going to keep repeating myself. I need to buck my ideas up or I'm going to sink fast."

"Exactly. Why keep repeating yourself? I know it's going to get on my tits, sooner or later."

Sara thumped Carla in the thigh. "Not what I wanted to hear, partner. Right, professional head on once again. One more visit, and then we'll get back to the station."

"The sister, right?"

CHAPTER 2

*A*lthough Paul had warned them what Amelia was like, Sara was still shocked to see her slouching around the house in her dressing gown at four-thirty in the afternoon, watching, of all things, daytime TV.

The young woman led them into the lounge which smelt musty. Sara resisted the temptation to stride across the room and open the window to let in some fresh air.

"Take a seat. I've been expecting you," Amelia said.

She puffed on a cigarette and stubbed it out in a bulging ashtray on the arm of the chair. Sara noted the half-full bottle of vodka sitting on the floor at Amelia's feet. It wasn't until she spoke again that Sara picked up the slight slur in her speech.

"Have you found her yet?"

"No, not yet. We're covering all the bases first, in the hope that something will come to light."

"I don't know what you expect me to do about it. The others consider me useless at the best of times anyway. I guess still not being dressed at this time of day is only proving them right."

"Not in my eyes. I've been told you're on medication. That can take a toll on a body, I'm led to believe. May I ask what's wrong with you, Amelia?"

"If you listen to my sisters, they'd tell you I'm lazy. But ongoing tests with my doctor, and he's come to the conclusion that I have depression plus a muscle-wasting disease on top of having Long Covid. I'm exhausted all the time. Without the tablets, I wouldn't be able to get out of bed most days, let alone function properly."

"I'm sorry to hear that. Are you telling me your family don't know about your condition or are you saying they choose to ignore it?"

"The latter. My sisters are both healthy and accuse me of pretending to be ill most days. Do they really think I want to live like this, day in and day out? Not having the strength or willpower to get out of bed most of the time?"

"Have you sat them down and explained your illness to them?"

"Yes, I've tried. They don't want to know, they're both wrapped up in their own little worlds to care about what happens to me. My mother understood. Saying that, my condition has worsened considerably since my parents' death. The doctor believes that grief has played a major part in the decline in my health. I wish I could get out of these blasted PJs now and again. Go to the park... ouch... I shouldn't mention that, not after what has gone on today. Never mind, you haven't come here to listen to me bang on about what's wrong with me, have you? Is there any news on little Mia? I wish I had the strength to get dressed and go out there and search for her. I would, you know, if I had it in me. Unfortunately, this is one of my bad days."

"It's okay. You mustn't put yourself down like that. If it's out of your hands, then there is very little you can do about it. Are you up to answering a few questions?"

"If you think I can help, then go ahead."

"Can you tell me if you have had any cause for concern with regard to Mia lately?"

She frowned. "I'm not with you. Are you suggesting that Eve or Paul could be behind my niece's disappearance?"

"No, nothing of the sort. Sorry, I probably worded my question wrongly in the first place. Have either of your sisters mentioned being uneasy about anything lately to do with Mia's well-being perhaps?" Sara kicked herself when she noticed Carla turn her way. She'd worded her question wrongly yet again, or so it would seem.

"Haven't you just asked me the same question but reworded it slightly? If you're suggesting Eve or Sandra, or Paul come to that, are behind Mia's disappearance, then you're seriously barking up the wrong tree, Inspector. They adore that child. Why would any one of them want to put her through such an ordeal?"

"I'm sorry. Let me try again, I wasn't insinuating that at all. What I'm trying to ascertain is whether either Eve or Paul had any concerns about Mia, or if they've mentioned someone was lurking outside the house or if someone had approached them out of the blue lately."

Amelia's mouth twisted from side to side as she thought. "I get what you mean now. No, they've never mentioned anything like that to me. I can't believe she's been stolen. What goes through someone's mind to snatch a damn baby, knowing how much it will need its mother at that young age? Don't bother answering. If you knew the answer to that daft question, you'd be out there rounding the frigging bitch or bastard up, wouldn't you?"

Sara nodded. "We're hoping that something will come to light sooner rather than later. At this time, we're going to be dependent on what comes from the conference that is due to air this evening. But anything the family can tell us in the meantime might prove beneficial to the investigation."

"I'm not stupid, Inspector, by the sounds of it, I believe you're casting a line, fishing for something, a clue, maybe angling for some dirt on the perfect couple. You think they're the reason the baby went missing, don't you? Come on, why don't you come right out and say it?"

"That's not true, Amelia, nothing could be further from my mind. Yes, I'm guilty of digging, but only for Mia's sake. All I'm doing is searching for the truth. In my experience, babies don't get snatched from under their parents' noses unless something is amiss at home." Sara felt Carla's gaze fix on her once more, and she cringed. Amelia had forced her arm. She had no reason or the intention to blurt out what had been going around in her head all day. Bothering her. Poking her with a four-inch needle even.

"My God, have you heard your-bloody-self? Jesus, if either Eve or Sandra, or Paul, heard you talking that way they'd swing for you with one of those demolition balls or whatever they're called."

"I'm sorry, I didn't mean to upset you. The only thing I'm trying to do is find out a plausible reason for Mia's disappearance."

"And it's logical that you should think the parents are to blame from the outset, is that it?"

"No, honestly, you're twisting my words, or maybe I'm simply not putting my point across very well."

Sara glanced at Carla for help. This time her partner avoided eye contact and kept her focus on the notes she'd been taking instead. A sinking feeling rifled through Sara.

Shit, me and my big mouth. Why do I keep putting my foot in it? Why can't I keep my thoughts to myself instead of steaming ahead and getting people's backs up? And why choose Amelia, someone suffering with mental health issues to air what's on my mind? Confused dot com at its finest. I need to get a grip before I put little Mia in yet more jeopardy, if that's possible.

"You shouldn't be here, saying all this. Are you even listening to me?"

Sara shook her head to clear her thoughts. "I'm sorry. Yes, you're totally right. Forgive me. I think it has been a long day and I'm guilty of voicing opinions that should never see the light of day. Shall we go, Sergeant?"

Carla glanced at her then and nodded. "I think it would be for the best."

"Hope things improve for you health wise, Amelia. Goodbye." Sara struggled to say more than that.

Outside the property, Carla let her have it. "What were you thinking back there?"

"At least wait until we're in the car before you try kicking my butt."

Carla huffed and marched towards the car. Sara pressed the key fob, and the doors clunked open. They got inside, and Sara raised a hand.

"Wait, don't lay into me as though I'm a bloody five-year-old."

"Give me one good reason why I shouldn't."

Noticing that Amelia was standing at the front window, watching what was going on, Sara started the car and drew away. She pulled up again at the top of the road, where she deemed it far enough out of Amelia's sight.

"What's wrong with you?" Carla asked. "Why did you bother going there if that's how you were going to behave?"

"I had no intention of saying what I did, it spilled out before I had a chance to stop it."

"That's bullshit, Sara, and you damn well know it. That poor woman didn't know what hit her, she was flummoxed, unsure what to say or do. As if she hasn't got enough on her plate as it is, you go marching in there accusing her sister

65

and brother-in-law of being behind their daughter's abduction."

"I didn't, not outright. Did I?"

"See, you don't know what you're saying half the time. You need to take a step back on this one, Sara, for your own good and for the baby's sake. How the fuck are you going to feel if something serious happens to the child? Have you considered that?"

"No. I don't need to take a step back at all. All I'm guilty of is searching for the truth. I don't know why you're getting so riled up. We always look into the parents in this kind of situation, it's standard procedure, for God's sake. Bloody hell, I've heard it all now. I think we'd better agree to disagree on this one. It needed to be said, I have no issues hitting her with the truth."

Carla folded her arms, and her leg jiggled. "Are you kidding me? You have no issues with grabbing that woman by the throat and…"

"Don't *exaggerate*. I did nothing of the sort, nor would I. Don't make me out to be some kind of monster."

"I think we'd better get back to the station and stop discussing this matter because my insides are tighter than a coiled spring, and I dread to think what will happen if we continue going over your failings."

"Charming, I wasn't that bad in there. You're blowing things up out of all proportion, as usual."

"Am I heck! Have you heard yourself?"

Sara chose to ignore her, squeezed her foot down on the accelerator and revved the engine a few times.

"Feel better for that, do you?" Carla snarled.

"Grow up," Sara bit back without engaging her brain first.

. . .

THEY ARRIVED BACK at the station to find a surprise waiting for them in the shape of a young woman. Jeff asked to see Sara for a quiet word in one of the rooms off the reception area before she had a chat with her.

"She came in about fifteen minutes ago. Said she heard something on the news about a baby being snatched and decided to come down here right away. She refused to tell me what she knows, ma'am, said she would only speak to the person in charge of the case and no one else."

Sara sighed and rubbed at her tired eyes. "Christ, not what I need at the end of a traumatic day. Okay, Jeff, is there an interview room free?"

"Number Two is available, set up and ready for you to use. Want me to ask a PC to join you?"

"No, I'm sure it won't be necessary. No, on second thoughts, yes please, then Carla can get some work done upstairs while I interview the woman."

In other words, I can't wait to get rid of my partner because she's suffocating me, or has been with the dreaded silence she's hit me with in the car.

"Consider it done. Want me to arrange for drinks to be brought in?" Jeff asked, his hand on the door handle, ready to leave the room.

"Not for me. You can offer her one, though."

Sara followed him out and had a word with her partner. "You go up. I'll interview the woman and join you and the rest of the team in a while."

"Huh! I can take a hint, even when you scrub around the issues. Have fun." Carla's hair swished as she turned and walked away.

Sara chose to ignore her partner's dismissive behaviour and fixed a smile in place. "Hello, you wanted to see me? I'm the SIO on the Randall abduction case." She felt foolish for forgetting to get the woman's name from Jeff.

"Mandy Fuller. I had to come. I've been going out of my mind with worry about that poor baby. I had to do something, to come here to see you. I've been pacing the floor at home, working myself up into a right state."

Sara's smile broadened. "Don't worry, let's get you into an interview room and you can tell me what's on your mind."

She punched her security code into the keypad, ensuring she hid what was being entered from Ms Fuller who was standing close behind her. Sara led the way down the long narrow corridor to Interview Room Two and offered the woman a seat. A few seconds later, a female constable joined them with a drink for Ms Fuller. She delivered the mug and then took up residence at the back of the room.

"What exactly have you come here to tell me today, Ms Fuller?"

"It's Mandy. I don't know how to say this, but I must. It's driving me nuts, knowing and keeping it to myself."

Sara frowned and tilted her head. "I find that coming right out and just saying what's on your mind is the best way. Do you want to give it a try?"

Mandy wrapped her shaking hands around the mug. The drink slopped onto the table. "Oops, I'm sorry. I'll get a tissue to wipe it."

"No need. I can do it." Sara plucked a couple of tissues from the box sitting on the edge of the table by the recording equipment and threw the soiled paper into the bin. "All done. You were saying?"

Mandy ran her trembling hand around her face, proving how nervous she was. "I have to tell someone."

"I'm listening," Sara said. She tried to hurry the woman along, keen to end her day. She'd been through the mill and back, her nerves in tatters after falling out with her partner on the way back to the station.

"It's about the baby."

"Yes, you've already told me that much. Why don't you take a deep breath and tell me what you saw?"

Mandy's gaze dropped to her mug, and she clutched it tighter, spilling yet more of her drink. "Oh my, I don't know what's the matter with me, I'm not usually this nervous."

"Take a sip of your drink and try to calm down." Again, Sara mopped up the spillage and disposed of the soggy tissue in the bin beside her.

Mandy managed to take a sip without further mishap and then sighed and placed her mug on the table once more. "I... I saw... I saw someone... someone take the baby. At least, I think that's what I saw."

Sara sat upright, her interest piqued for the first time in hours, and flipped open her notebook. "You did? Are you sure?"

"It was in the area that you mentioned, on the estate behind the park. I was walking my little Mimi, she's a French bulldog, cute as a button, she is. Anyway, I came out of the park and saw a man putting a pram in the boot of his car and then he put the little one on the back seat, just laid it down, didn't bother strapping it in or anything, which raised my suspicions, kind of. He drove off. I didn't think any more about it until I heard that a baby had been abducted on the news."

"I see. Didn't you notice the woman lying on the ground... the victim? The mother of the baby?"

"No. I'm ashamed to say I didn't. I saw the man in the car and then decided to turn back and take the other route around the estate."

"And you missed the mother lying on the pavement?" Sara repeated to clarify what the woman was telling her.

"Yes, that's what I said. It's no good you looking at me like that, as if you don't believe me, then that's your problem, not

69

mine. It is what it is. I was busy watching the car, my focus remained on that as it drove away."

"And did you get the number plate down?"

"No, should I have? I didn't know there was anything wrong with the scene and that the man was up to mischief at the time, so why would I take his number plate?"

"Okay, perhaps that was expecting too much of you. What about the make and model of the car?"

"It was a dark-green Toyota Auris, you know, one of those hybrid cars. I recognised it because I've been looking at buying a new car lately, wanting to be greener in my choice, and that model caught my eye."

"That's great news, so you're a hundred percent certain about it then, yes?"

"Definitely. I wouldn't state I was, unless it was true."

"Good, now we're getting somewhere. Did you see what direction the car went?"

"Not after it left the estate, no. I went in the opposite direction, remember?"

"What about a description of the man?"

"Now you're testing me." Mandy closed her eyes and nodded. "All I can do is take a guess at his size, I have nothing to compare it to as such."

"That's good enough for me."

"I'd say he was around six feet, maybe an inch or two taller, not any shorter than that."

"His hair colour? Or was he bald?"

"Oh no, he had hair. It was on the darker side, not black, but a stronger brown than a mid-colour. Does that make sense, or am I guilty of talking in riddles?"

It's either brown or black, love, nothing in between. "No, that makes perfect sense to me," Sara replied and braced herself for the pimple breaking out on her tongue. "Any distinguishing features?"

"Such as? Can you give me a clue what type of thing you mean?"

"Did he walk with a limp, have one arm?"

"Oh, I understand now. No, nothing that I can think of."

"What sort of clothes was he wearing?"

"Oh, that one is easy. Blue jeans, the kind that are faded on the thighs. He had bulging thighs by the way, as though he worked out. I couldn't tell what his upper body was like because it was covered in a dark baggy hooded sweatshirt. Hang on, if he was up to no good, why didn't he bother disguising himself by wearing the hood up?"

"That's a good question and one I'd be interested in learning the answer to. Shoes?"

"Trainers. They were white, had a go-faster stripe on them. Would they be Adidas or Nike ones?"

"I think we might luck out with that, many manufacturers use the go-faster stripes these days, but we'll investigate all the same. Going back to the car... Were there any distinguishing features about that? A missing alloy perhaps, a sticker that caught your eye on the window or boot of the car?"

She paused, raised her chin and thought over the answer but ended up shaking her head. "I'm useless, aren't I? I'm sorry, I guess I'm not as observant as I profess to be. I've always considered myself to have an eye for detail. Shows what I know, eh?"

"It's fine. If the whole incident happened at breakneck speed then you mustn't beat yourself up about it. We have more than enough to be going on with, I assure you. Was there anything else you wanted to add?"

Mandy started to speak several times but stopped, hesitation preventing her from completing her sentence. "Umm... I was wondering how the mother is. Or don't I have the right to ask?"

"Of course you do, especially after supplying us with such important information. She's in hospital. She was attacked from behind. They believe she has concussion. Obviously, she's very concerned about her daughter's safety and wants to be reunited with her as soon as possible. With this new and valuable information, I'm hoping that day will come very soon."

"Oh dear, how dreadful for her. To sustain a bad injury and to lose her baby on the same day, or during the same incident, should I say?"

"We're at a loss to understand the abductor's motive. All we're hoping and praying for is that they keep the baby safe from harm. Silly statement in the circumstances. I hope this person can handle the demands the infant throws at them. Babies tend to cry a lot, and if you're not used to dealing with them, it can lead to a mountain of frustration."

"Oh yes. I agree. My sister had twins. How she coped with their demands, day in and day out, I will never know."

"Double the trouble, I should imagine. Was there anything else you need to tell me?"

"I can't think of anything. Is that it then? What will you do with the information? Or is that a daft question?"

"Not at all. I definitely won't be sitting on it. I'll get it actioned immediately. A couple of members of my team are trawling through the CCTV footage around the park right now, so it'll be good to have some definitive details for them to search for. I can't thank you enough for going out of your way to come here to see me today. I'm sure we'll be a few steps closer to finding the culprit and the baby, thanks to the information you've shared."

"That's great. What I was hoping to hear you say. Give my regards to the parents, especially the mother. Sorry she had a whack to the head and was unable to protect her baby. Life sucks at times, doesn't it?"

"It does indeed. I'll show you out."

Mandy finished off her drink, threw her cup in the bin, then rose to her feet and followed Sara back up the hallway and into the reception area. They shook hands.

Sara gave her a card. "If you think of anything you forgot to tell me, don't hesitate to get in touch, day or night."

"Thank you, Inspector, I'll be sure to do that."

Sara waved her off and, now with a renewed spring in her step, she trotted up the stairs to the incident room. "I've got some news for you all." Her gaze fell on Carla, but her partner kept her focus on her computer screen, intentionally avoiding eye contact. Sara growled inwardly, but outside she shrugged and addressed the rest of the team. "I've been downstairs interviewing a witness to the abduction."

That caught Carla's interest. She glanced up and folded her arms, waiting for Sara to share the details of what went on during the interview she hadn't been required to attend.

"This woman, Mandy Fuller, was walking her dog. She'd come out of the park, presumably taking the same exit as Eve and Mia. She strolled around the estate and stumbled across a dark-green Toyota Auris. A man was putting a pram in the boot when she laid eyes on him. Then he put a small baby in the back seat of his car. No safety seat or the like in sight, which is more than a little concerning."

"Bugger, if he didn't think of the child's safety when transporting her, then how is he going to cope caring for her every hour of the day? We all know how much time and effort babies take to keep them content," Christine said.

"I know, that's a major worry in my opinion. Still, we can't dwell on it, not now. What we need to do is focus on the information she has given us. Craig, you and Barry search the cameras again. This time I need you to try and find the Auris for me, unless you can recall seeing one already during your former search?"

"Nothing is coming to mind, boss. We'll get on it now."

"Thanks, see what you can do for us. It's all we have at this moment, so it's imperative we get something from it."

"Has the woman gone?" Carla asked out of the blue.

"Yes, why?"

She shrugged. "I wondered, that's all. Did she say anything else?"

"Yes, she gave me a rough description of the man. Damn, I forgot to ask how old she thought he was."

Carla raised an eyebrow as if to say that wouldn't have happened if you'd bothered to allow me to sit in on the interview.

"You have something to say, Carla?"

Her partner pointed at her chest and shook her head. "Me? No, nothing."

"Good. I'll note down the description she gave me on the board, should anyone be interested in it."

Sara did that and then went into her office. In need of hearing a friendly voice, she rang Mark. "Hello, you. Are you nearly done for the day?"

"Sorry, no. I was about to ring you. I've got an emergency coming in, one that requires surgery tonight. I don't think I'll be home before midnight."

"Ouch, cat or dog?"

"A cat. It got dragged under someone's wheel and is a right mess, touch and go whether it survives. I haven't seen the state it's in yet. The owners rang earlier and are on their way in now."

"I'll keep the poor pussy in my thoughts."

"You're an angel. I think it's going to need all the help it can get by the sound of it. How's your day been? I caught the tail end of your press conference about an hour ago. I was about to give you a ring, see if you're all right when I took the call from the owners of the cat. I've been setting up the operating theatre ever since."

"Don't worry about me, you have enough on your plate. It's imperative you keep a clear head. I might work late here then, get a takeaway and catch up on some paperwork instead of sitting at home, all alone."

"You're forgetting about Misty, she'll need some company after being by herself all day."

"Damn, you're right. Shame on me for not considering my pussy."

Mark chuckled. "Umm... nope, I'm not rising to that one. Ouch, did I just say that?"

"You did. You're as bad as me and you don't even realise it."

"Glad to hear the smile in your voice, I was beginning to think you were on a downer today."

"I am, or should I say, I was until I spoke with you. One of those frustrating days where nothing seems to go right."

"You put far too much pressure on yourself, love. I bet you haven't had a lunch break today, have you?"

"Can you remind me what one of those is? I seem to have forgotten. I'm fine, don't worry about me. You concentrate on putting that pussy back together again. Give me a ring, let me know how the operation went when you can, after you've informed the owners, of course."

"I'll be sure to do that. I hope the rest of your day proves less stressful for you, sweetheart. I've gotta fly. I think the owners have arrived."

"Good luck. I'll be thinking about you and that poor pussy you're about to put back together again."

Mark laughed and blew a kiss down the line.

Sara placed her mobile on the desk and stood to take in the view. The mountains were covered in low cloud, matching her dreary mood. Moments later, a knock on the door disturbed her.

Carla poked her head into the room. "Is it safe to come in or are you likely to bite my head off?"

"Me? When have I ever done that... er, without good reason, I should add? Come in, as long as you've got a cup of coffee with you."

Carla held the mug up and entered the room. She handed Sara her drink and muttered, "I hate it when we fall out."

Sara put her mug on the desk and held out her arms. "I think we both need a cuddle."

Carla slipped into her outstretched arms and hugged her tightly. "See how astute you are?" She withdrew from the hug and placed her hands on Sara's arms. "How are you holding up?"

Sara shrugged. "I thought I was doing all right until you asked. No, I'm fine, you worry too much."

"It's an emotional case that I fear is getting to both of us."

"It sure is. I can't say I've ever felt this way during an investigation before. The only words I can dig up to describe it is *emotionally wrought*."

Carla nodded. "And we've only been on it less than twelve hours."

"That's my biggest concern. We, or I, shouldn't be feeling this way this far into it. I can't figure out why."

"Why don't we wrap things up and go home, put this to bed for the night and look at it with fresh eyes in the morning?" Carla suggested on a sigh.

"I'm torn. Half of me wants to hang around and deal with any calls that might come in after the news airs, and the other half of me wants to go home, make the most of having the house to myself for a change, and possibly lock myself in a dark room with a bottle of gin."

"House to yourself? Why?"

"I rang Mark. He's got an emergency operation on a cat this evening, doesn't think he'll be home before midnight."

"Oh crumbs, poor Mark. The joys of being a great vet, eh? You can always come home with me and we could tuck into a takeaway."

"And look over a bunch of cold cases, like you and Des usually do?" Sara sniggered.

"And there you go again, mocking me."

"I'm doing nothing of the sort. I'll hang around here for a few hours and then go home to be with Misty."

"Fine, if I can't persuade you to do otherwise. Do you want me to stay behind for an hour or so, to keep you company?"

"No, there's no need for both of us to man the phones. Go home, get some rest while you can."

"I'd rather be here with you, but if that's the way you want it, who am I to argue with you?"

"Exactly. There really wouldn't be any point in you arguing with me, you know I always win."

Carla groaned and left the office. Sara took a final glance at the hills beyond that were clearly visible now that the clouds had lifted. She envied them, sensing her mood wouldn't be dispersing anytime soon.

She joined the rest of the team and had a quick word with Craig and Barry to see if they'd spotted the car on the footage. They hadn't. They both seemed as downbeat as her. She rubbed their arms. "Come on, guys, I know you've given it your all. There's always tomorrow. Go home, block all of this out of your minds for the evening, and we'll start over in the morning."

"Wait, you haven't asked for a volunteer to man the phones this evening. I'm up for it," Craig replied.

"No, I'm going to stick around myself tonight. Now get out of here before I change my mind, that's an order."

The team drifted off over the next ten minutes.

Carla was the last to leave. "Are you sure you don't want me to stay with you?"

"I'm positive. Now go."

"I'll see you in the morning then, you know where I am if you want or need a chat."

"I do. I won't tell you again, skedaddle, leave me to it."

Once Carla had left, the silence hit Sara much harder than she could have anticipated. She spent the next ten minutes bringing the whiteboard up to scratch with the list of people she and Carla had spoken to throughout the day. In between making notes, her gaze coasted over to the main phone on Christine's desk, and she cursed it for remaining quiet.

At ten, bored out of her mind, and nearly falling asleep at her desk after completing copious amounts of paperwork that she had neglected, or simply hadn't had the time to deal with over the past few weeks, she finally gave in and went home. Mark hadn't rung her. She resisted the temptation to call in at the vet's on the way home. When she walked through the front door, Misty virtually threw herself into Sara's arms.

Sara snuggled into her fur and Misty purred noisily in her ear.

"Hello, sweetheart. I'm so sorry I've left you for so long. Let's see what treats we can find for you." Removing her shoes and jacket, whilst juggling Misty from one arm to the other, she swept into the kitchen, switched on the kettle, and then fed Misty and swooped to take care of her litter tray, which was messier than normal. Not surprising, considering how long her furry companion had been left alone during the day.

She'd just completed her chores and made her drink when the front door opened and Mark announced his arrival.

"Hey, you're earlier than you thought you were going to be. Is that a good or bad sign?"

"All good. Two mended broken legs, both clean breaks. I pity the owners trying to keep that little one quiet for the next six weeks while she heals."

"I know how tough it would be to keep Misty amused. What do you fancy to eat?"

"Nothing. I grabbed something earlier, don't worry about me. You look exhausted." He gathered her in his arms and kissed the top of her head.

"I can't deny it. I decided a takeaway wasn't for me but I'm going to need something or I'll wake up starving during the night. I've only been in twenty minutes or so myself. What if I fix us a tray of cheese and biscuits? We've got an unopened bottle of red in the cupboard, we could take it up to bed with us."

He raised an eyebrow. "Who am I to argue with such an excellent idea? Can I help?"

"You can let Misty out for me, something I haven't got around to doing yet. I prioritised the need to clean her tray which was a bloody mess and stinking the place out."

"I'm not surprised." He kissed her and then crossed the room to open the back door to let Misty out.

She trotted out and under his watchful gaze, had a quick wander around in the dark and came back in, all before Sara had managed to get out the plates and sort the biscuits for their supper. She completed the task, and Mark carried the tray upstairs while she locked up and gave Misty an extra treat or two.

"That's all you're getting out of me tonight. My guilt has seeped away now, Munchkin."

Misty wound herself around Sara's legs, and she gave in and dropped another couple of treats on the floor for her.

Mark was undressed and in bed by the time she made it into the bedroom.

"Eager, aren't you? I think I'm going to jump in the shower first."

"I pondered the same then decided against it. This cheese is calling to me."

Sara laughed and wagged a finger. "Leave me some. I won't be long."

She sought out a pair of fresh PJs and slipped into the bathroom. Tying her hair back so it didn't get too wet, she washed away the stresses of her day, or so she thought. They emerged again when Mark asked her how her day had really gone.

"I can tell how much this case is affecting you. I'm here if you need to chat."

Sara buttered a cracker, cut off a slice of Wensleydale with apricots and sighed. "I think I'm all talked out for the day. It's true, this one has well and truly got under my skin. I stayed behind, hoping that the phone would ring off the hook, but not a single call came in. I know the estate is a bit tucked away but I was hoping for a bit more, I must say."

Mark reached for her hand and squeezed it. "Didn't anything come from the house-to-house enquiries?"

"Nothing at all. I did have a witness call into the station this afternoon."

"A witness? To the abduction?"

"That's right. She gave me a description of a man who she believes took Mia."

"Well, that's a positive lead, surely?"

"It might have been, if Craig and Barry had found the car she described on the cameras in the area. They didn't. There-fore, we're back to square one."

"Shit! That's a shame. Did the woman try to stop the man from taking the child?"

"No, she didn't see anything wrong with the scene at the time. It's only since she heard the appeal go out this afternoon that things slotted into place for her."

"So she saw the man loading the baby into the car, but what about the mother?"

"I asked the same question. The mother was lying on the pavement, and she didn't notice her when the car drove off. She told me that she had already set off in the opposite direction by the time the man got in his car and drove away."

"Sounds odd to me. But if that's what she said, then who are you to question her?"

"It's the lack of leads that is drenching me in frustration."

"I don't know how you're coping. I'd be kicking people around the room, demanding answers if I were in your shoes, not that I'm insinuating that your team aren't doing their best."

"They are. We all are, but with little to nothing to go on, it's hard to get the investigation going. That's why I've been disappointed with the response I've received from the appeal today."

"Yeah, you'd think someone out there would have noticed something out of the ordinary, someone walking around with a baby they didn't have last week. It's not rocket science, is it?"

"No, but I suppose it shows what our society has become. The lack of community spirit, looking out for each other, is really noticeable to coppers."

"Lack of bobbies on the beat?"

"Yeah, that old cry. Still, who are we to question how the Force prefers to use the funds it is handed out every year?"

They tucked into their cheese and biscuits, the conversation turning less intense.

"Dad and Margaret are off on their travels again soon."

"There's no stopping them, is there? Where are they going this time?"

"They're venturing up to the west coast of Scotland. Dad's always wanted to visit that area, but Mum didn't fancy it, so he lucked out."

"I do envy them, taking off at the drop of a hat. Getting away from it all when things start to get on top of them."

"Truth be told, I do, too. Something to look forward to in our retirement, eh?"

He faced her and smiled. "It can't come soon enough. Sod this going abroad, being held up at the airport for hours on end, I'd much rather stay in this country, explore what the British Isles have to offer."

She wiped away the crumb at the edge of his mouth and nodded. "I'm gradually coming around to that idea. I suppose a lot of people are thinking the same way, since the pandemic. Less flights will definitely have an impact on the environment."

"Something to be considered, the rate at which global warming is increasing."

Sara's eyelids drooped. "I think I'm going to try and get some sleep now. Goodnight, darling."

Mark removed the tray from between them, placed it on the floor, and then switched off the light. They snuggled up, and it wasn't long before Sara drifted off to sleep, mentally exhausted by the day's trials and tribulations.

CHAPTER 3

*T*he constant crying was driving her insane. She'd tried everything she could think of to silence the baby, only to fail. The temptation was there to thrash the life out of it, but where would that get her in the end? She had a deadline to meet, another three babies to snatch yet.

Christ, how the fuck am I going to cope with more than one, especially if this one starts them all bawling their heads off? Keep calm, Fiona. Deep breaths and talk to the brat nicely. I need to dig deep for any maternal instinct that is buried within.

She tried cooing at the baby, which seemed to bring about a brief respite to her ears, only for the child to realise that Fiona wasn't her mother and to start crying once more. In the end, she left the distressed baby in the bedroom and closed the door on it. Although she could still hear it breaking its heart when she ventured into the kitchen to prepare her breakfast, it was good to have a reprieve from the noise. How the fuck did people put up with a child stressing like that, twenty-four hours a day?

"Nope, it's not for me. In my eyes, the world would be a much better place to live in without ankle biters to share it with." Civilisation would be enriched for it, too. "Let's face it, it would soon die out." She let out a deranged laugh at the thought of the last few people surviving when everyone else had died. Just like in one of those bizarre sci-fi films she detested so much.

She prepared herself toast and a mug of coffee then went through to the lounge and switched on the TV. The local news came on. She nibbled on the toast, slathered in peanut butter, and watched yet another rerun of the appeal go out, her eyes boring into the soul of the officer in charge of the investigation.

"You think you've got problems now, DI Sara Ramsey, you ain't seen nothing yet." She let out another laugh and flicked channels to catch the news on the other station.

Not long after, she checked on the baby once more. It was still driving her nuts with its crying. She tried to settle it, but peering into the cot only appeared to make the situation worse. She left the house a few minutes later, relieved to get away from the constant ear-bashing the infant was intent on giving her. Driving into the city centre eased the misery she'd been suffering since she'd abducted the pain-in-the-arse baby. She had a target in mind, a location at least, not a specific target as such. There was a small row of shops close to the centre she had been staking out lately. Only last week she'd gone there and witnessed dozens of women pushing either prams or pushchairs with older infants perhaps on their way to a playgroup in the area.

She could take her pick, the choice being plentiful around there. Fiona parked in the pharmacy car park and waited patiently for the opportunity to come her way, no nerves cloying at her insides. If anything, she felt the excitement brewing within.

What a warped fucker I am.

She laughed as a possible target left her car in a hurry.

The woman stopped a few times to look over her shoulder, then she disappeared around the corner, possibly going to visit the pharmacy. Intrigued, Fiona got out of her car and jogged across the tarmac. She peered through the back window, and there, staring back at her, was a baby girl, larger, probably a few months older than Mia. Fiona tried the door handle and it clicked open. She punched the air and peered over her shoulder to see if the mother was on her way back. She wasn't. Heart pounding, Fiona removed the baby from the car and quietly shut the door again, avoiding giving the mother a clue that anything was wrong before she got close to the vehicle. The baby screamed in Fiona's ear. She jiggled it and cooed, a big smile on her face.

Great, yet another noisy fucker to contend with. It's a good job the deadline is fast approaching. Not sure I could put up with dealing with a handful of screaming brats under my roof for more than a few hours.

She shuddered as the image of the woman who had given birth to twelve kids ran through her mind. The article had appeared in the local paper the previous month. Fiona had contemplated trying to find the woman to steal her youngest. It wasn't likely that she'd miss one, would she?

The baby's crying intensified. One minute she was staring into her mother's angelic features, and the next, the devil's face had replaced it.

"There, there, sweetheart. You're going to be all right with me. We're going to take a little ride in a nice big car. You're going to love it."

She cast a nervous glance around her every now and again, breathing out a relieved sigh when the coast remained clear until she jumped back into her car. With the baby safely fastened into the back seat, she drove away from the area. She beamed, grateful and gladdened that the job had been carried out with ease. She returned to the house and placed the two babies, who had around six months between them, in the same cot. Being in close proximity to each other seemed to put the babes at ease, and they both fell quiet.

Fiona went back downstairs and poured herself a much-deserved glass of wine. So what if it was only eleven in the morning? Who was there to stop her from enjoying herself? Her mobile rang. Her contact's name lit up the screen. "Hi, how's it going?"

"All good at this end, just checking in to see what progress has been made."

"I've told you before, there's no need for you to check up on me all the time. I've got two babies out of the four, so I'm on course."

"Jesus, I would have thought you'd have collected them all by now. You're putting yourself under immense pressure to snatch the other two kids."

"That's my problem, not *yours*. Did you see the first one mentioned on the news last night?"

"I did, that's why I'm ringing you, to see how things are going and if the baby was unharmed during the abduction."

"It was. I've told you before, you need to trust me. I'm a dab hand at this type of thing. Trust should be a two-way street."

"Yes, so you told me when you came to see me last week. I expected more, though. Are you sure you're not putting yourself under pressure, leaving everything to the last minute?"

"It's all in hand. You worry too much."

"Yes, that's been said before. I have good reason to worry, there's a lot at stake. Mess this up for both of us, and this could be the end of our little arrangement before it has had a chance to get off the ground."

"And you think nagging me is going to put everything right? Not that anything was wrong in the first place. Give me space to do the job you've entrusted me with. I won't let you down."

"Make sure you don't, there's too much riding on this that will affect our future undertakings. Are the kids being fed properly? All their needs being seen to?"

"What do you think? I'm sensing a lack of faith in my abilities here."

"Nonsense. I'm bound to check if the babies' needs are being met."

"They are. Now, let me get on with things. The clock is ticking, and you ringing me every five minutes, all right, that's a bit over the top, but you know what I mean, well, it's only going to hamper my progress."

"I can take the hint. If any issues arise, I want to know about them ASAP."

"You'll be the first to hear. I'll be in touch in the next few days." Fiona didn't wait for a response, she ended the call, seething that her partner felt the need to check up on her.

How dare she? Maybe I should jump up and down on her back now and again, ensure she's doing all she can to keep people interested.

She cringed and went through to the kitchen to check if she needed any nappies or formula. She had a feeling she was running low and should have stopped off at the supermarket on her way home. Half a pack of nappies lay in the cupboard and a third of a tin of formula. She'd need to nip out and pick up more supplies soon. First, she would get the babies changed and fed. It had been a while since she'd changed Mia. Had she done it this morning before going out? She couldn't remember. Not ideal, considering she'd been put in charge of the babies' safety and care.

She waved the problem aside and made up a couple of bottles of formula which, along with the nappies, she took upstairs and saw to the babies. She entered the room, relieved that the two of them appeared to be getting on better now they had company. Now she could understand why people had more than one child in quick succession. Although, on the flip side, if either of the babies cried, it was bound to set the other one off. Definitely a no-win position to be in. Still, long may the silence and the babies' willingness to play with each other continue. It would make her job so much easier if it did. She fed Mia first. She didn't have a clue what the other baby's name was... yet. No doubt she'd find that out soon, through the media.

CHAPTER 4

*W*hen Sara and Carla arrived at the pharmacy on the outskirts of the city, they found the distraught mother sitting in a chair, rocking back and forth, a bottle of sports drink on the floor beside her.

Sara showed her warrant card to a man in his thirties, hovering close to the woman. "Mr Bengali?"

"Yes, that's right. I'm the one who rang you. This woman has had her baby stolen, you must help her."

Sara got down on one knee beside the woman and placed a hand on her leg. "Hello, are you up to telling me what happened?"

The woman's gaze connected with hers, and she whispered, "Someone took my baby. What more can I tell you?"

Sara smiled. "You can tell me your name."

"It's Dana Pratley." She let out a large breath and shook her head. "I was in a rush. I'd just been next door to the surgery. I had an appointment with my doctor. He gave me a prescription to help me sleep because I'm exhausted. My daughter keeps me awake most nights."

"Okay, I'm sorry to hear that. Then what?"

"I left the surgery, put my daughter, Samia, in the car, and then I came in here to pick up my prescription. When I returned to the car, my daughter was missing."

"Someone had broken into your car and taken her?" Sara asked, needing clarification.

She shook her head. "No, in my haste to get Samia home, I must have left the car unlocked. Why? Why was I so stupid? Wait, don't I know you? Weren't you the officer on the news yesterday, after that baby went missing? No, don't tell me... don't say it."

Sara clasped Dana's hand tightly and noticed how much it was shaking. "Let's not jump to conclusions, not yet. Did you see anyone hanging around when you returned to your car?"

"No, there was no one out there. You have to believe me, I didn't intentionally leave the car unlocked. I would never usually do that. My child's safety is paramount to me, always has been. I must have had a lapse in concentration. I know I'm blaming this on my lack of sleep, but some days I genuinely don't know whether I'm coming or going. Please, you have to find my baby girl. Have you found the other child yet?"

"Not yet, but we're out there searching for her. Don't worry, we'll find them both. You stay there, have a drink. I want to have a word with the pharmacist." Sara stood and gestured for Carla to stay with Dana while she crossed the shop and sought out the pharmacist who had left them and returned to his duties. "Hi, can I have a quick chat with you, Mr Bengali?"

He left the open section at the rear of the shop and joined her in the corner, away from prying ears. The man had tanned skin and spoke with a slight accent.

"Of course. This is terrible. I hope you can help her. She's a regular in here, buys all her baby formula that I sometimes have on special offer. Sorry, I'm wittering on. What do you need to know?"

"Can you tell me what happened out there from your point of view?"

"I was busy in here, putting the latest batch of patients' prescriptions together that had come through from the doctor's next door. I heard a scream out back, in the car park, and didn't think twice about going to investigate. I found Dana in a heap on the ground, next to her car. The back door was open, she had her arms inside the car and her head resting on the back seat. She started sobbing. I raced over there to see what was wrong. That's when she told me her baby had been stolen. She was in a terrible state. It took me a while to encourage her to come inside. I gave her the only drink I had available. I don't drink tea or coffee and try to discourage my staff from drinking it, too, so we don't have any on the premises."

Sara got the feeling the man was talking non-stop because he was nervous speaking with a police officer. She did her best to put him at ease with one of her disarming smiles. "Did you see anyone lingering out there? A car driving off perhaps, anything along those lines?"

"No, I neither saw nor heard anything. Only Mrs Pratley screaming, begging to be reunited with her daughter. It was a harrowing incident to witness. I wish I could do more to help her. I wanted to call an ambulance, but she insisted I should ring the police instead. I had it in my mind to do it anyway. I heard and saw the appeal you put out about the baby that was abducted yesterday and put two and two together. I made a note of your name, in case I overheard anything in the shop that I could report to you. Do you think there's a connection?"

"You're very well organised, Mr Bengali, not everyone would think to take down my name and to contact me at the first sign of trouble. Your prompt action to get in touch might be what we need to find the baby quickly. Do you have any cameras inside or outside the property?"

"Yes, I have them outside, covering the car park." He tutted and curled his lip. "How foolish of me not to think about that. I can check the footage for you."

"If you wouldn't mind, that could give us the vital information we need to begin our investigation."

"Do you want to view it with me?"

"Lead the way."

He took her to a room off to the side which consisted of a couple of monitors, a desk, a chair and a filing cabinet. He wheeled the chair in front of the monitors and hit a few buttons on the recording machine positioned below it.

"I'll go back to ten minutes before I heard Mrs Pratley scream."

"Yes, that'll do, we can always go back further if we discover anything of interest."

Sara watched him work wonders with the machinery with her heart pounding. *Please, please let there be something on here we can latch on to. I fear time is against us on this one. Why is someone kidnapping these babies?* "I forgot to ask Dana how old Samia is, do you know?"

"She's around a year old. The baby taken yesterday was younger, wasn't it?"

"That's correct. Six months. It's all very perplexing, as you can imagine."

"Did the other mother see the person who took her baby? Or shouldn't I be asking such awkward questions?"

"You're okay. No, the mother was struck on the back of the head. Her baby was stolen while she lay on the ground unconscious."

"Is she okay? Concussed, I should imagine."

"That's right. She's still in hospital, recovering from her ordeal. Devastated, she is. She has every right to be as well."

"And both abductions took place during the day. That's the part I'm struggling to get my head around," Mr Bengali said.

"Ditto. It would seem the abductor isn't averse to taking a risk or two."

"Ah, here we are." He selected the button to pause the machine and pressed play. "This is Mrs Pratley returning from the doctor's and putting her child in the back of the car. Oh dear, she does seem to be distracted. She's juggling her purse, her keys and her prescription. I know she hasn't been sleeping very well lately, hence the need for the tablets she picked up. You can see she forgot to lock the car. I haven't seen the indicators flash, have you?"

"No. I feel for her. She's going to be riddled with guilt for days, weeks, or possibly months to come, if we don't locate her daughter soon." Sara returned her attention to the screen and saw a woman wearing a jogging suit, the hood of which covered her head, approaching the car. "Great, there's no chance of making a proper identification, not with her face and head covered. Let's see what happens here first, and then perhaps you can rewind it five minutes or so. Maybe we'll be able to see her arriving, whether by car or on foot."

"Yes, that's a good idea. Let me see what I can do for you here first."

They observed the proceedings in silence as the woman seized the opportunity that had materialised. She opened the back door and blatantly removed the child from the car then walked back in the direction she'd come from.

Mr Bengali took his cue from Sara. She nodded, and he rewound the recording to five minutes before the woman appeared on the screen.

"There, two cars arrive in quick succession. Can you go back further and maybe pause once they come into view?"

"Of course. I hope this helps. I'd like to be of further assistance to help out my distraught customer."

"We're both doing our very best for her. Stop, there." One vehicle entered the car park and drove out of view of the camera, and then the other vehicle entered and parked close to the entrance. "Can you focus on the first car? Go back again. Let's observe it pulling in and see if we can make out who the driver is or what they're wearing to clarify if it might be the woman who took the child," she said, speaking as if she was talking to Craig who was usually in charge of viewing any and all CCTV footage to do with an investigation.

"I'll do it now. Yes, I think she's wearing the same jogging suit, is that what you call it? Or leisure suit perhaps?"

"Either, it really doesn't matter. Yes, bottle green. Can you home in on the number plate of the car?" The camera zoomed in on the blue Ford Focus, but the number plate was obscured with mud. "Great, looks like someone was keen on covering their tracks."

"Does that sort of thing happen a lot? I should imagine that it does."

"Yes, more than you'd think possible. There are some very crafty criminals around these days."

"Sorry I can't do any better for you."

She touched his arm. "Don't be, you've done your best for us, that's all we can hope for in the circumstances. Can I ask you to run a copy off for me, please?"

"I'll do that for you now, then I must get back to work. If I miss ten minutes out there, I can spend the rest of the day chasing my tail. Is that the right term?"

"It is. Have you been in this country long?" Sara picked up on his lack of confidence with his English.

"Many years, over twenty now. Sometimes the language still flummoxes me, but most of the time I cope pretty well."

"Put it this way, I think you speak better English than some of the natives I have to deal with, especially when I arrest them."

They both laughed. He prodded a few keys and inserted another disc, then ran the recording again and paused it after the part where he appeared from the back of the building and ran across the car park to see if Dana Pratley was all right.

"I like to think I did my best for her. Hopefully the footage will come in handy for you in your search for this revolting woman. She's despicable if she thinks she can get away with stealing another woman's baby."

"She'll be punished, once we catch up with her, I can promise you that."

"I hope this helps, I really do. I'm trying to imagine what Mrs Pratley must be going through, and I have to tell you that I'm struggling."

"Maybe it's best if you try not to think about it. What's done is done. All we can do is try to prevent this from happening to someone else. Having this footage to hand, I can call another press conference and ask for the general public's help in identifying the car and maybe the woman, you never know your luck. We have to think positive. I'd better get back out there, make sure Mrs Pratley is as well as can be expected. Thank you for taking good care of her and for calling the station to report the crime."

"It was my duty, Inspector. I'm sorry the footage wasn't better for you."

"Honestly, we'll get it analysed by Forensics. It's surprising what they can pick up once they run it through the system."

"I'm sure. I wish I had been able to offer her more help

and could have prevented the abduction before this woman got away with the baby. Sorry, I might have muddled up my words there, I tend to get a little mixed up when my feelings are taut or I'm a little anxious."

"You're doing fine. I understood exactly what you were saying."

He handed her the disc he'd placed in a plastic case, and they left the room.

"How are you doing?" Sara asked Dana upon her return.

"I'm confused. I keep running things through my mind. I don't think I've ever left my car unlocked before, so why on earth did I do it this time? I'll never be able to forgive myself. Shit... I need to tell my husband. He's going to be livid. He's bound to blame me for not looking after her. Yet another nail in our relationship."

Sara frowned. "Oh? Care to enlighten us?"

"We're separated. He couldn't stand being around Samia when she cried. She's not a bad baby, let's say she has her moments. I told him to get out, rather than listen to him constantly ordering me to keep her quiet. What the heck? Some men don't have a clue how to deal with children. They must think babies have an on and off switch. Anyway, if I don't inform him, he's the type to use it against me when the divorce is heard in court, not that he'll be fighting for custody, he's told me he wants nothing more to do with her."

"Sorry to hear that. He sounds an absolute arsehole, I mean, charmer." Sara smiled. "Maybe you're better off without him if that's what's going on in his head. Do you want me to contact him? I will, if you'd rather not have to deal with him."

"No, I think that would only make matters worse, him being contacted by someone from the police and me not bothering to fill him in. I can't help thinking that I'm between a rock and a hard place. Damned if I do, not that he's likely to offer a sympathetic ear or anything, and damned if I don't, and he finds out that Samia has gone missing. Jesus, can my life get any bloody worse? I thought I had it all, a great marriage, a baby on the way that we both truly wanted. A week after giving birth, and the bastard started staying out, going to the pub on the way home from work every night. I put up with it for so long and tackled him about the issue. That's when he admitted that he couldn't stand being around Samia and he wasn't sure that he even loved her."

"Ouch, that must have come as a shock."

"It did. He told me first thing in the morning as he was about to walk out the door. I was too stunned to retaliate. Instead, after he left and the shock turned to anger, I spent the day packing up his things. I also called in a locksmith to change the locks on the front door and left all his possessions outside on the lawn. I kept an eye open for him. He eventually got home at nine forty-five and was furious. His fury went up a level when I refused to open the door to talk to him. He ended up throwing a brick through the window. That's when I was forced to call the police. They came out and arrested him for causing criminal damage."

"Okay, I can look that up, see how it was left. Did you press charges?"

"I told him to fix the window. If he did that and agreed to leave Samia and me alone, then I would be willing to drop the charges against him. He did. I haven't seen hide nor hair of him since. That was about eight months ago."

"Some men just aren't worth it, are they? Have you been coping by yourself all this time?"

"Yes. My mother looks after Samia when I work part-time. His mother chips in now and again, determined to keep in touch with her granddaughter. I don't mind, she's really nice. Unlike her son. To think I loved him and he promised me the world when we got married. He's the one who insisted that we should start a family right away, and then, he walked away from us, emotionally at first. I had to kick him out."

"Are you saying you feared for your daughter's safety?"

"It was getting that way. What harm can a little human that size do to a fully grown man? He seemed petrified of her most days. Too scared to touch her, talk to her, and he did nothing but ignore her. I didn't know he had it in him, to be that bloody callous. I suppose you don't really and truly know a person until they've experienced one of life's greatest challenges... birth, death and moving house are the three main ones, aren't they?"

Sara nodded. "That's truer than most people seem to believe. Is there any chance he can be behind your daughter's disappearance?"

"God, don't say that. I don't think so." She paused, and her gaze fixed on the shelf of hair products in front of her. "Now you're making me question myself. He wouldn't, would he?"

"You'd better give us his place of work and his address. I think we need to have a chat with him, just in case."

Carla produced her notebook and pen and flipped it open to a clean page, then handed it to Dana.

"Take your time. If you can jot down the details, that will be our first call once we drop you home."

Her hand shook as she wrote down the information, and then she handed the book and pen back to Carla. "I'm okay to drive. I've got my car here. I would much rather you get on with your job, Inspector. I don't need babysitting, what I need is for you to find my baby."

"Don't worry, we're going to begin our investigation in earnest now. We've already issued an alert. Mr Bengali has been kind enough to supply us with CCTV footage that could prove vital. We'll get the ball rolling with that and hit the road, providing you're okay?"

"I am. Yes, I want you to get out there. There's no need for you to worry about me, I came out of this unscathed, I'm just missing my baby. The sooner you start looking for her the easier my mind is going to be."

"Don't worry, leave it to us. Can you jot down your own address for me as well?"

Carla handed the notebook and pen back to Dana who added her details to the page and returned the items to Carla.

"Take care," Sara said a second time. She shouted thanks to Mr Bengali who had by now returned to work.

He waved and gave her the thumbs-up.

Sara and Carla left the pharmacy and raced towards the car.

"What did you see on the footage?" Carla said once they were buckled up.

"A woman approached Dana's car and took the child. She wore a jogging suit with the hood up, so it was impossible to make her out. I got Mr Bengali to rewind the disc, and we saw two cars arriving. One parked in sight of the camera, the other did its best to avoid it. But we could make out it was a blue Ford Focus."

"And you reckon that one belonged to this woman?"

"Yes, at least I'm hoping it does, and before you ask, it was impossible to get the number plate as it was covered in mud."

"Shit! Why isn't anything simple these days?"

"The criminals are getting smarter, thanks to the wonders of modern TV, but we say that every time."

"You're not wrong. Hey, we've got one thing going in our favour, though." Carla faced her and pointed a finger.

"And that is?"

"You said it was a woman."

"Yeah, are you forgetting what Mandy Fuller told me

during her interview? She said she saw a man get into a car and drive off with the first baby."

"Crap, I had forgotten. Is there any chance the woman in the footage could be a man?"

"Anything's possible, especially as she ensured her features were hidden from the camera. I'm going to drop the disc off to Forensics on the way back, they can analyse it for us. I'll tell them we're unsure whether the culprit is male or female, see what they can work out for us."

"Here's another suggestion you're not going to like."

"What's that?"

"What if we're looking at two separate culprits? A male and a female, maybe a double act who are taking it in turns to snatch the children. Or something even more puzzling to consider... what if this woman saw the appeal go out and we're dealing with a copycat."

Sara groaned, and her head flopped forward and smacked against the steering wheel. "Don't confuse the issue any more than is necessary, please. I can't even contemplate that being what we're up against, Carla."

"Okay, ignore me then... at your peril."

Sara sat up and stared at her. "Did you have to add the last part?"

Carla laughed. "Get over it. We need to keep our options open, nothing is set in stone just yet."

"I know, that's what's bugging me. Okay, let's head over to see Dana's husband or soon-to-be ex, see what he has to say, if anything."

"Ha, I'm sure he's going to have plenty to say when he hears the news. Whether he loves the baby or not, having two coppers show up at his place of work is going to spoil his day and cause some severe embarrassment with his colleagues."

"Listen to you, how do you know that? Are you the new oracle?"

"Common sense. I was at the front of the queue when the Lord was handing it out."

Sara coughed and muttered, "Bullshit!" She slipped into gear but before she got the chance to pull off, her mobile rang. It was the station. "DI Ramsey."

"It's Jill, boss. I wanted to let you know that Becky dropped off the footage you were expecting. She apologised, said when she viewed it, she saw nothing out of the ordinary on there. Craig took the liberty of going over it and he said the same."

"Oh well, it was worth a try. Thanks, Jill."

"No problem."

Sara ended the call and got the journey underway once more. She took a shortcut en route to avoid the build-up of traffic which usually occurred at that time of day.

The garage was larger than Sara had anticipated. There were several cars up on ramps over inspection pits. The sign outside had given her the heads-up that it was an MOT centre.

Sara showed her warrant card to the blonde woman filing her nails behind the reception desk. "DI Sara Ramsey, and this is my partner, DS Carla Jameson. Would it be possible for us to have a word with Adam Pratley?"

"Adam? Is he in some kind of trouble?" She tucked the file into the long tube of her desk tidy and jumped to her feet.

"Is he around?" Sara asked, ignoring the woman's question.

"I'm going to have to run this past the boss first. I'll get him."

Sara smiled tautly and nodded. "You do that. If you can make it snappy, we'd appreciate it."

The receptionist tutted and knocked on the door behind her. A man's voice bellowed the name Cassy.

She opened the door and poked her head around it. "Sorry to trouble you, Nigel. The police are here. They want a chat with Adam. I told them I'd have to get the go-ahead from you first."

"What shit has he been up to now? If it's not one thing, it's another. What am I paying these guys for? To bring sodding trouble to my door daily? I've had it up to here with them. Just let them see him and be done with it, Cassy, it's not like we can stop them, is it?"

"Okay, boss. I didn't want you…"

"I've got to get on, my accountant will be on my back if I don't get this paperwork to him by the end of the day. I'll leave the police in your capable hands. Don't make them too comfortable or we'll never get rid of them."

"Yes, Nigel. Sorry to disturb you. Where shall I put them? In the rest room? What if the others come in for a break?"

"Tell them not to. They've got fifteen minutes to see him, that's all, got that?"

"Understood."

Cassy returned to the front desk and opened her mouth to speak.

Sara raised a hand to stop her. "It's okay, we heard everything."

Cassy's cheeks flared. "Sorry if he came across as rude. We've had a bit of bother with a couple of the lads this week, and he's on a bit of a downer with them. He's also got hassle at home with his wife and teenage daughters, so life is a touch traumatic for him, shall we say?"

"We all have our crosses to bear, it's called life. It doesn't matter. If we can get on… I'm aware that he's only allowing us fifteen minutes to see Adam."

"Yeah, sorry about that. We've got cars booked in and

coming out of our ears today, and he's keen to ensure things run smoothly for the rest of the week because he's off to the Caribbean on Sunday."

"Ah, that explains it. It's all right for some."

"Yeah, I haven't had a holiday in five years. We just can't afford it. My fella and I have been saving up to get married."

"Congratulations, it's not cheap these days. Have you thought about eloping?"

"It's cropped up during conversations, but our families would be furious if we went ahead and took a trip up to Gretna."

"Just do it. What can they say once the deed has been done?" With time marching on, Sara regretted getting involved in a subject that didn't concern her. "Sorry, it's not for me to interfere. If you can get Adam for us? That'd be great."

"Yes, yes, I'll do it now. You'll need to see him in the rest room. It's the first door on the right. You make yourselves comfortable, and I'll go and fetch him."

She rushed out of the main entrance, and Sara and Carla shifted locations in her absence. The rest room was as Sara expected it to be, an utter mess. Cans of beer and pop littered the small table along with smelly takeaway cartons, mainly burger containers, no doubt from the outlet across the road.

"Jesus, why don't men seem to have the ability to clean up after themselves?" Sara grumbled.

"Some men," Carla corrected. "Mark and Des don't appear to be tarred with the same brush, thankfully. It stinks in here." She crossed the room and opened the window above the sink to see if that would give them the fresh air needed to conduct the interview without needing to vomit.

"Nice try, not that it's going to make any difference," Sara said.

The door opened, and Cassy walked in with one of the

mechanics. His grey overalls had oil splotches here and there, and his hands were black and grimy. He went to the sink and wiped some of the grime onto the dark-green towel hanging up next to the sink. Washing made no difference to his hands whatsoever.

Sara produced her warrant card again, and Cassy left the room.

"I'm DI Sara Ramsey, and this is my partner, DS Jameson. Thanks for agreeing to speak with us."

He threw himself into one of the plastic chairs and spread his legs out, taking up most of the room around the table. "Like I had a choice. What do you want?"

"Where were you between the hours of ten and eleven this morning?" Sara asked. She had an inkling what his response was going to be.

He held his hands out to the sides. "Er... here. I've got witnesses as well. We've been hard at it all day. Why?"

Sara cleared her throat and took a step closer towards him. "We were called out to an incident on the other side of the town, near the doctor's surgery in Widemarsh, do you know it?"

"You're talking about my surgery, I take it? Of course I bloody know it, why? What am I supposed to have done? Because if anyone is telling you I've been up to no good, I want to know who it is. I'll go round there and give them what for."

"You're not doing yourself any favours making threats like that."

"I wasn't, it's a frigging *promise*. How would you like it if someone dobbed you in to the police and lied?"

"You don't know why we're here, you're assuming that's the case."

"Isn't it? Look, instead of bloody wasting my valuable time, why don't you tell me what's going on here?"

"As I said, we were called out to an incident this morning that took place outside the doctor's surgery. Actually, it was in the pharmacy car park."

He frowned and fidgeted in his seat. "Is there a point to you telling me this?"

"The incident involved your wife, Dana."

He sat upright. "I know who my wife is. Believe me, some days I wish I didn't, but what does this have to do with me?"

"I'm getting to that. Your wife visited the surgery then put your daughter in the back of the car before she filled her prescription at the pharmacy next door."

"And? Can you get to the rub of why you're here? What my wife does no longer has anything to do with me. You probably know we're heading for the divorce courts."

"We do. The problem is, when your wife came out of the pharmacy and returned to the car, your daughter was nowhere to be seen."

He jumped out of his chair, his bulky frame filling the room. Sara stood back against the wall, and Carla did the same.

"What the fuck? Are you telling me someone took my kid?"

"Yes."

"And you're here to come down heavy on me, is that it? You think I'm behind this?"

"Not necessarily. We have procedures we need to follow. You're in a dispute with your wife, and your child has gone missing. We're bound to come here to try to get to the bottom of this."

"Fuck, you can't be fucking serious. My kid is missing, and I'm the first person you have on your radar? Jesus, you should be out there looking for her, not frigging hounding me. I've got nothing to do with this. I would never hurt that child, that's why I walked away in the first place."

Sara stared at him. "You're not making any sense. Care to clarify what you mean by that statement?"

"I meant that if I'd hung around, I fear what might have happened. Lock me up for being honest, but don't come down here frigging believing that I have something to do with this. Why didn't my wife take more care of the child? Did you ask her? She was in sole charge of the kid, and yet here you are, frigging questioning me. Something ain't sitting right with me. You've got this all arse about face. Why is it you lot only consider what the women say and want in a relationship? The courts are the same, always coming down on the side of the mother. I'm not contesting anything she wants because I know I wouldn't be able to handle the child. Sure she's a nightmare, constantly crying all the time, but that doesn't mean that I would hurt the kid." He stopped pacing and fell back into the chair and covered his face with his hands. "Taken. What the fuck? How? Why?"

"Your wife has been under immense pressure lately. In this instance, I fear lack of sleep might have affected her judgement. She placed Samia in the back of the car which she left unlocked. She's devastated."

He lowered his hands and sneered. "So she should be. That woman has put me through hell the last year or so, calling me an irresponsible bastard, and she does this! What the fuck! And now here you are, pestering me because you probably think I have something to do with my daughter's disappearance. That frigging sucks. I'm telling you, nothing could be further from the truth. I've distanced myself from Dana and Samia because I found it too hard to handle. I miss them but I know too much water has gone under the bridge and there's no way back for us."

"That doesn't have to be the case. If you truly love your wife, then showing her support when she's at her lowest ebb I'm sensing will get you back in her good books."

He laughed. "You think? She despises me, and who can blame her? I turned my back on them when she needed me the most. The truth is, I don't believe I was ready for fatherhood. I was way out of my depth. She had already bonded with the child by the time she came out of the hospital, there was no way in for me."

"Nonsense. Of course she will have a bond with the baby, she carried it for nine months, it's part of her."

"Hey, I had a hand in her production as well, you know."

"I'm not saying you didn't. Your little swimmers did their job, and it was up to you to be there for Dana and Samia once they were back home with you."

"That was the plan, but then the kid started kicking off and shit... all I could think of doing was running for the hills and staying there. I got used to having time on my own again, and that's when I decided it would be better to cut all ties with them and knock the marriage on the head. I couldn't find a way back, even if I wanted it."

Sara shook her head. "Men! Your problem is that you raise the defences and us women find it impossible to break them down. You give the wrong impression to begin with, and things snowball into something else very quickly, and before you realise it, it's too late to turn back the clock, in your opinion. Well, I have news for you, women have more brains than you give us credit for. We can see what's going on, and by the time we reach out and try to change things, it's often too late."

"That's just it, it's too late, it's been like that for a while now. Dana detests me for the way I have treated the pair of them over the past year."

"It's never too late, not if the willingness is there and you still love your wife."

"I do. Maybe, oh, I don't know anymore. I'm sensing there's no way back for us. But enough about us, what's going to happen now about my baby? I hope you have patrol cars out there searching the area. Hey, wait a minute, did I hear something on the news yesterday about another baby going missing?"

"That's right. This is the second incident of this nature that has come to our attention in the last few days."

"And? Did you find the other kid or not?"

"Not yet. The investigation is ongoing."

"Christ, now you have two kids missing, and one of them is mine. I still can't get used to saying it. To me, all ties had been cut with Dana and Samia. I was getting on with life being a bachelor again."

"As I've already suggested, if you reach out to your wife now, it can go one of two ways. You won't know which way until you try. What have you got to lose?"

"My self-respect, my dignity."

Sara raised an eyebrow. "You're never going to get another chance like this one, I promise you."

He ran his hands through his short dark hair and looked at her. "You reckon?"

"Absolutely. It's got to be worth a shot."

"I'll give her a call, tell her I'm here for her if she needs me."

Sara shook her head. "I'd go round there in person if I were you. Face-to-face encounters are far better than dealing with major issues over the phone or through a solicitor."

"You're right. I'll see if the boss will let me have a few hours off this afternoon to be with her. He's a family man and always having a go at me for not manning up and avoiding my responsibilities. But, that's not going to bring Samia back, is it?"

"It's going to go a long way towards putting everything right between you and your wife again, take my word for it. Taking action now, while your daughter is missing, will help lay the groundwork for when she returns, if you're serious about making another go of it with Dana. However, a word of caution, if I may?"

He narrowed his eyes and gestured for her to continue. "Go on."

"You need to remember they come as a package, you can't have one without the other. Babies settle down, eventually, or so I'm told. I don't have kids myself, so I can't speak from experience."

"I think I realise that now. I'll make this work, for all three of us, if that's what Dana wants. I suppose I'd better get in touch sooner rather than later."

"Good idea. Okay, we'll leave you to it."

"Inspector, I want to thank you for coming here and making me see sense today."

"All part of the service. Take care of yourself, your wife and your daughter, once we get her back to you."

With that, Sara and Carla left the rest room and accompanied Adam back through the garage under the watchful eye of his colleagues.

Back in the car, Carla tapped Sara on the left thigh and said, "You're an old softie at heart."

"It was clear to me how much he was suffering. Men need a good shake-up now and then before they throw their lives away. He'd regret it the rest of his life if he didn't take action now and let the case go through the divorce courts. Men need to be more emotionally attached to their relationships, stop holding back to save face."

"Yeah, you're right. Sometimes they have trouble dealing with what's right there in front of them. It's true what they say, for some folks."

"What's that?"

"Men are from a different planet to us, and it shows."

"Again, I'm not about to disagree with you. Okay, that's

our good deed done for the day. We'd better get this disc dropped over to Forensics now and get back to the station. Thinking about it, I think I probably need to alert Jane, get her to arrange another press conference for us."

"Want me to do it while you drive, or do you want to swap places?"

"It's fine as we are. I'll ring Jane, and you can take over. She'll be putty in your hands. In fact, put it on speaker, and I'll pitch in if necessary."

Carla's eyebrow shot up. "If that's the case, you might as well talk to her yourself."

"Sorry." Sara grinned. "Yes, I might as well, you know what a control freak I am."

Carla rang the number and began the conversation with Jane. "Hi, Jane, this is Carla Jameson, Sara Ramsey's partner."

"Oh yes. Everything all right, Carla? What do you need?"

"Far from fine. Sara's asked me to give you a call about arranging yet another press conference to do with the case we're working on."

"Shit! Is this about the baby who went missing?"

"Yes, except now, we have two babies missing."

"Oh crap. Of course, let me make a few phone calls and get back to you in ten minutes."

"Thanks, Jane. You're a star."

"Maybe, let's see if I can pull things together first. Send my regards to Sara, tell her to keep her chin up. I know what effect the first case was having on her."

"Don't worry, she's worked through all that now and is back on top form again, she has to be. Do your best for us, speak soon."

"Leave it with me, Carla."

"Thanks, Carla," Sara said. "She'll pull out all the stops for us, she always does. Even more so when there are two babies involved. No one likes to consider kids being in danger, do they?"

"So true."

Sara pulled into the car park and tore through to the Forensic lab. She was greeted at the door by a technician with a mop of red hair and a matching fuzzy beard.

She explained the urgency behind her visit. He took the disc from her and said that he would personally deal with it himself and that she should expect a call from him in no later than twenty-four hours.

Sara smiled and thanked him, then flew out of the building again. "Right, let's get back to the station. I don't suppose Jane has rung back, has she?"

"As it happens, yes. She's made arrangements for the press to arrive at four. It's the earliest she could do it."

"That's fine. It's coming up to two now. Let's stop off at the baker's and treat the others to lunch. I bet they've been all hard at it and haven't had time to eat, like us."

She stopped off at the regular baker's the officers at the station frequented and came away with half a dozen sandwiches. "I resisted the urge to buy a bunch of cream cakes."

"I can pick up a fruit cake or something from the shop on the corner."

"Good idea. Lunch isn't the same without something sweet to finish it off."

Sara parked in her usual spot and carried the bag of sandwiches upstairs. Carla set off for the shop, and they met up back in the incident room. Sara was halfway through her sandwich when she received a call from Dana Pratley.

"Hi, Dana. How's things?"

"I was going to ask you the same. How did you get on with Adam? I bet he was livid that I'd given you his address, wasn't he?"

"Not really. Well, in all honesty, he was to start with, but he soon calmed down. Like most men, I think he's misunder-stood." Sara winced, sensing she had said too much.

What if all Adam told me is a blatant lie? I can't say anything to Dana, just in case he backs out of doing what he said he was going to do.

"Oh, what gives you that impression?"

"Nothing in particular. I suppose years of experience of reading people is in my favour."

"Ah, yes, I should imagine you get to deal with all sorts of people in your job. Did he blame me?"

"Not really. He was concerned. Look, I might as well tell you. They're snowed under at work today, but he's going to see if he can get some time off. He's intending to come and see you, you know, to show his support."

"Oh no. I'm not sure how I feel about that. After all this time, how am I going to react to him being in the same room as me?"

"I think you're going to have to set your feelings aside and take all the support he's willing to offer you at this time, Dana. Samia is his child, too."

"Yeah, I know, but he walked away from her, and from me, and now he's probably going to come round here and lay the law down."

"I don't think that'll be the case at all. Give him a chance. See how things go. You're in this together. We can only do so much at this end, but you're going to be relying on friends and family to help you through this ordeal. I think he should be a part of this."

Silence filled the line.

"That's going to be so difficult, including him after all he's put me through and actioning the divorce proceedings as well. I'm out of my depth here."

"It's something you're going to need to deal with. I know it's not going to be easy with all that's gone on." Sara stopped short of telling her to forgive him and to be willing to give him another go. That wasn't her place to interfere in their lives. She'd advised Adam well enough for him to make the next move if his sole purpose was to keep his family together.

"How can I deal with what he's going to throw at me when all I'm concerned about right now is getting Samia back home where she belongs?"

"My advice would be not to stress about it. Let things go at their own pace. All I can tell you is that he was very upset that Samia had been taken, we all are."

"It's a relief to hear that, especially after he's been so vile towards her. Maybe it's his guilty conscious at play here. Unless the alternative is true."

"Alternative?" Sara perched on the desk behind her.

"Could he be behind her disappearance? What if he paid someone to take her, to punish me for taking him to court?"

"I genuinely don't think that's the case at all. Try not to dwell on things too much. See how the land lies when he finally comes to see you."

"Okay. I'm a mixed bag of emotions right now, he'll have to accept that, except he won't. It's always been his way or the highway. I can't see that changing anytime soon."

"Give him and yourself a chance. Let's be honest, neither of us knows what lies ahead of us at this stage. I'm going to have to go now. Oh, one more thing, I've called a press conference for this afternoon."

"Oh. Do you want me to attend?"

"No, there's no need. If nothing comes of it then we may have to rethink things and possibly you and Mia's mother can consider putting out personal pleas to the public and to the kidnapper. Sometimes they work, other times they can hinder an investigation's progress."

"I'll do whatever is necessary to get my child home. I'm a strong woman, Inspector. Okay, it might not have come across that way earlier on, but when the need arises, I am prepared to do anything and everything to get my baby back."

"Hopefully it won't come to that, Dana. I'll be in touch soon."

"Good luck, Inspector. Wait, can I give you a photo of my baby? I could send it through."

"Yes, you read my mind, I was just about to ask for one." Sara gave her the number to send it to and ended the call, sensing they were going to need all the luck they could lay their hands on, and more, over the next few days.

CHAPTER 5

$\mathcal{M}$aking her way down the stairs to chair yet another press conference, Sara felt a headache brewing. *Damn, why didn't I pop a couple of paracetamols before tackling the journos?*

The second she laid eyes on her, Jane appeared concerned. "Hey, you look rough. Everything okay? I thought it was strange when Carla got in touch with me earlier."

"I'm fine. The start of a headache coming on, no big deal. I've just been cursing myself for not taking some tablets before coming down here. I don't suppose you have any on you, do you?"

Jane smiled. "You'd be surprised what I carry in my handbag. Ta da!" Jane produced a foil packet of tablets and gestured for Sara to hold her hand out. She popped two out of the foil and into the palm of Sara's hand, then dipped into the conference room and returned with a glass of water from the jug she'd already set up in the room.

"It's still filling up in there, so there's no rush if you want to delay it a minute or two. It might not be a bad idea and will allow the tablets to start working."

"Except now I'll get even more stressed because you've told me there's a roomful of journalists getting ready to pounce on me." Sara pushed the pills down the back of her throat with her finger, making herself retch, and then washed them down with a large gulp of water.

"Blimey, I hope you don't need to take tablets that often if it's that much torture for you?"

"It is, but thankfully I don't need to rely on them that often. Bugger, I didn't make any notes for the occasion. I'm going to have my back against the wall from the outset in there."

"Stop stressing. I recall you've always managed it in the past, despite your reservations. Why should this time be any different? It won't be, so try to chill. You should be used to holding one of these by now."

"You'd think so, wouldn't you? Not this time, though. Come on, shall we venture in there? Time's a wasting for the babes that are missing."

Jane gave her a quick hug to reassure her and then led the way into the room and onto the slight stage that she had set up in readiness. Sara took her glass with her, sat at the table in front of the bulging crowd and topped up her glass from the half-filled jug beside her.

"How are you holding up?" Jane leant in and whispered.

"Let's get this over and done with. I'm ready, if you are."

Jane didn't think twice, didn't need to prepare herself. She turned to the journalists and said the relevant spiel which settled the room down. Sara was in awe of her confidence as usual. Ever the professional, able to turn it on with a click of her fingers. Sara couldn't help but feel a tad envious of her colleague as she spoke. Then Jane handed the conference over to Sara who felt anything but confident.

"Yes, thank you, Jane. I'm sorry to have to call you back here so soon. The investigation we discussed the other day is still ongoing, we're out there searching for little Mia Randall night and day. Unfortunately, I have to share the devastating news with you that there has been a second baby kidnapped within Hereford today."

The crowd mumbled and fidgeted in their chairs en masse. Jane had to call for order in the room before Sara could continue. Only after the last journalist quietened down, did Sara speak again.

"This time the child reported missing is twelve-month-old Samia Pratley. The little girl was stolen from the back of the car while her mother was within a few feet of her."

"Did the mother take her eye off the ball, Inspector? Is that what you're telling us?" a journalist Sara had come to expect a tough time from demanded to know.

"No. I don't want to go into details about that. What's important is that we are now hunting the whereabouts of two babies. We need your help to find them. The person responsible is snatching these children in broad daylight. That takes a certain amount of guts to carry out."

"Do you know what their motive is yet, Inspector?" a woman in the third row asked.

"Unfortunately, we don't, not at this stage. The second abduction took place in the pharmacy car park in Wide-marsh. I'm calling on the public to come forward if they saw anyone unusual hanging around the pharmacy or the surgery next door between the hours of nine-thirty and eleven this morning. If you did, please contact the number at the bottom of your screen immediately. There is something very sinister going on that we need to stamp out, and quickly."

"Aren't you going to tell mothers and fathers out there to be vigilant?" the first journalist said before Sara had a chance to add anything else.

"Given the chance, that's exactly what I was about to say. We can't emphasise enough the need for everyone to be vigilant, and if anything seems off, we have officers manning the lines. Report any suspicious incidents to us, and we'll check them out right away."

"Any suspicious incidents?" the same obtuse man asked. "Surely you need to be more precise, don't you? Otherwise you're going to be bombarded with calls, referencing all sorts of crimes apart from the ones you're most interested in, aren't you?"

Sara seethed inside, annoyed that he should pick up on her mistake but combatted his objection the best she could. "If you give me a chance to finish a sentence now and again."

Jane knocked her leg against Sara's as if advising her not to waste her breath on the damned man.

"Moving on, we mustn't forget about Mia Randall in all of this either. The last press conference we aired, sadly produced very little. I'm just going to recap that case, if you'll allow me to."

Pages flicked, and the journalists put their heads down to take notes. Sara recapped the information she had imparted before and then turned her attention to the new case they were working on. "Someone must have seen something. If you know anyone who travels past, or works in the Wide-marsh area, please share this information with them just in case they don't see the conference themselves. We need to find these children swiftly. They're far too young to be away from their mothers at this early stage in their lives. It's up to all of us to ensure these babies are returned to their parents as soon as possible."

"We need the police to pull out all the stops as well, Inspector, don't we?" the same antsy journalist asked.

"Believe me, all available resources are being utilised on this investigation. There are more designated patrols out there, circulating the area. Don't be afraid to stop an officer if you feel you have any information you want to share with us."

"Is that why I saw four officers in the reception area, laughing and joking just before this conference started, Inspector? Is that your interpretation of throwing all your resources at this investigation?"

Sara glanced sideways at Jane who took the hint and drew the conference to a close.

"Thank you all for coming at such short notice, we appreciate the efforts you're making, and I'm sure it will prove beneficial soon, once the babies have been located and returned to their parents."

Sara was the first to rise from her seat, her gaze drawn to the journalist who had pounced and refused to let go. He grinned broadly and raised an eyebrow. Sara's stomach churned with the man's audacity.

I can do without you making my job a whole lot worse, you effing cockwomble.

Jane caught Sara by the elbow and steered her off the stage and into the anteroom. "Hey, you broke the first rule of press conferencing."

"You're going to have to remind me what that is, Jane."

"Never allow the arseholes to get to you."

Sara stared at a spot over Jane's shoulder until tears blurred her vision.

"Sara, come on now, it wasn't that bad in there."

"Wasn't it? I let the babies down. I'm continuing to let them down during this investigation. Yes, we're giving it our all, but if the general public isn't supplying us with any leads, we're screwed. I feel screwed, in more ways than one. That journalist was vile and enjoyed attacking me. Lacking in compassion or understanding of the job we're trying to do here. It isn't easy. Why don't, or can't, they realise that?"

"He set out to push your buttons and he succeeded. Truth

be told, his boss has probably pulled him over hot coals during the day and he's come here to take it out on you, and if I'm honest with you, you bloody allowed him to."

Sara shook her head, and in that instance a couple of large tears slipped onto her cheek. She was too stunned to wipe them away. Jane yanked her across the room to the stack of chairs in the corner. Jane arranged two of the chairs and pushed Sara into the one opposite her.

"Hey, what's going on here? I thought you'd got past all of this."

"I thought I had, too, but nothing could be further from the truth. Between you and me, I'm telling you this because I know it won't go any further. I can't help feeling out of my depth with this investigation. Do you know how many frigging calls I received after the last conference was aired?"

Jane shook her head.

"One. Okay, it turned out to be a witness who saw baby Mia being kidnapped, or so she thought. But that was about it, she gave me fuck all in the way of leads, no number plate to the vehicle. All right, she supplied us with the make of the car and a description of the man. My guys have extensively searched the CCTV footage in the area before and after the time the incident took place and found absolutely zilch. I hate dealing with dead ends, it does nothing for the morale of the team. We need something to cling to."

"That's the older case, what about the new one? You really didn't give out much information on that one."

"Because that rude fucker unnerved me."

"You've got to learn to rise above it. I know this investigation is taking its toll on you, but if you crumble, Sara, where will that leave the parents of the missing children? They're relying on you to hold it together. You've got this, whether you believe that or not at this stage. You're doubting what is going on in your head; you're the only person questioning your abilities. There, I've said it."

Sara reached for Jane's hand and grasped it. "Thank you, you always talk a lot of sense. I'm sorry if you feel I've let the side down in there today."

"You're guilty of twisting my words. I didn't say that, nor would I. You're the thorough professional in my opinion, always have been and always will be. The only drawback I can see that caused you any concern today was going in there unprepared. You've always got a handful of notes with you when you attend one of these. Why not today?"

"Stress. I've had a lot to contend with during the day. Speaking with the parents who are separated, doing all I can to bring them together so they could comfort each other during this horrendous time."

"That's commendable but has probably taken up a lot of your time today. You shouldn't have to do that, Sara. That, to me, screams that you have pushed yourself too hard and gone above and beyond what's expected of you. I'm not surprised you're an emotional wreck."

"Thanks." Sara smiled through the tears. "I wouldn't have quite said it that way myself."

"Oops, sorry. You know what I mean. Your emotions have been put through the wringer already today, only to be confronted by that nasty piece of shit in there. I'm not surprised it has ended the way it has. Come on, this isn't like you. You need to bounce back soon or…"

"Sink. You might as well tell it how it is and be done with it." Sara smiled again and removed a tissue from the packet she kept in her pocket and blew her nose.

"Stop it. You need to take a step back if you're suffering, Sara. Carla seems a quietly confident partner to me, someone you can rely on in a crisis. *Use* her. Let her take over some of your duties to ease the burden on your shoulders. I can't even begin to understand what pressure you're under during a normal investigation, let alone one that now has two children missing. It can't be good for the soul, love. You're going to need to learn how to switch off now and again."

"If I do that, then the kids could be getting further and further away from us. We have no idea what we're dealing with. Why these kids are being abducted within a few days of each other. I forgot to mention that we caught the abductor of baby Samia on disc. The image wasn't great, it's with Forensics now."

"See, that's great news and probably something you should have shared with the journalists, although I can understand your reluctance to do so."

"That's just it, it wasn't down to reluctance, more down to my forgetfulness."

"Ouch, in that case, you really do need to let your partner take up some of the slack for you, Sara."

"But if I do that... all I'll be doing is letting the parents down."

"And what's the alternative then?"

Sara sighed and buried her head in her hands. "I won't be able to do it, relinquish the reins." She released her hands and stared ahead of her at the floor. "I'm getting the impression that this isn't any ordinary investigation. The leads are proving impossible to come by. As far as we know, we have a male and a female kidnapper on our hands, if the proof is to be believed. The witness from the first case said a man abducted Mia, but the evidence I've witnessed with my own eyes has revealed that a woman was responsible for Samia's abduction."

"So a double act? It doesn't bear thinking about. What do you think will be their next move?"

Sara shrugged. "I wish I bloody knew. The truth is, I

don't. Carla seems to think that we might be dealing either with a twosome or possibly a copycat."

Jane gasped and shook her head. "That's horrendous either way. I suppose that's the danger of putting out a press conference, it might spark an idea in someone's head to jump on the bandwagon."

"Precisely. We won't know which scenario is true until more facts emerge. That's the frustrating part about working a case like this and why we're so reliant on the public guiding our way."

"I totally get that. Sara, if there's ever anything I can do to help, you only have to give me a call."

"I know. You've had my back more times than anyone else I've ever worked alongside, apart from Carla, of course, it would be wrong to keep her out of the equation."

"I knew what you meant, and it's good to hear. You're one of the better inspectors, if not the best, that I've worked with over the years, Sara. You give your all to every investigation and never let the general public down from what I can see. These cases are different because you feel there's so much more at stake than any of the other cases you've been involved with lately."

"Ain't that the truth?" Sara produced another tissue and dabbed at her eyes. "I'd better get back to it and allow you to get on with your day. Thanks for caring, Jane, and thanks for all you do for me. I'd be up shit creek without you by my side."

"You wouldn't at all, but thanks for saying it all the same. Are you going to do what I said and hand over the reins to Carla?"

Sara gave her one of her not-in-a-million-years kind of looks and smiled. "I think we both know the answer to that one. I'll be fine, it's the frustration leaking out. If I can find a way to tap it, everything should be great."

"Good luck with that mission. Don't forget I'm on the end of the phone if you ever need to have a chat."

"Much appreciated. Thanks again, Jane."

They stood and returned the chairs to the stack and then shared another brief hug.

Jane patted Sara on the back and whispered, "You've got this. You're one of the strongest women I know."

Sara stepped away from her and smiled. "I must keep telling myself that. See you soon, although not too soon, I hope."

Sara retuned to the incident room to find several long faces that reflected her own. "Craig, can you sort everyone out with a coffee, please?"

He bounced out of his chair and was swiftly followed by Barry.

"I'll help hand them around. How did the conference go, boss?"

"It was a tough one. The journalists quite rightly had a go at me for allowing yet another baby to be abducted. We need to right that wrong, guys. Let's brainstorm, see what we can come up with over a coffee."

They did that for the next few hours, mostly going round and round in circles. Finally, Sara gave in to her weariness and called it a day. Once again, Craig volunteered to man the phones that evening. This time, she took him up on his offer.

"If you're sure Jenny won't mind?"

"She won't. She's out tonight teaching a yoga class anyway, so it's no big deal, boss. This way, I can trawl through the CCTV footage again, see if we've missed anything we shouldn't have in the Mia Randall case."

"You're a good man, Craig. Tell Jenny from me that she's lucky to have you... umm... on second thoughts, maybe you shouldn't tell her that, if she's the jealous type."

He laughed. "She isn't, fortunately."

The team drifted home. After dropping a tenner on Craig's desk for him to buy a pizza, Sara left the station with Carla.

"How are you? You seem defeated," Carla said once they reached the cars.

"About sums it up. I'm tired, I'm sure a good night's sleep will be the cure that's needed."

Carla cocked an eyebrow. "I don't know who you're trying to kid, but it sure isn't working on me. Go home, get some rest, Sara. We've got a few new ideas to try out in the morning. We won't be able to do that if you're knackered."

"I know. I'll take a couple of sleeping pills if I need to. Goodnight."

CHAPTER 6

"*D*amn, I knew I should have stuck around last night. What have we got, Jeff?"

"I'm sorry, you looked so knackered last night, I was dreading telling you this morning."

"Don't worry about it. I can catch up on my sleep anytime. Let's concentrate on getting these babies back home to their families."

He nodded and handed her a slip of paper. "Another baby stolen first thing this morning. I took the call myself at seven-thirty. I've sent a couple of patrol cars out to the location. Reports are coming in that they've drawn a blank."

"You should have rung me straight away. Where's the mother or father now?"

"The mother is with her family. She was on her way to her mother's house after falling out with the boyfriend last night. She snuck out of the flat at first light. That's when the kidnapper attacked her. She was walking down by the river, laden with bags. She told me the pram tipped up, and while she gathered the bags and tried to distribute them better, someone ran at her from behind and pushed her in the river."

"What the fuck? You really should have rung me, Jeff."

"Sorry, ma'am. I realise that now, but after seeing the state you were in yesterday, well, to say I was torn would be an understatement."

"I appreciate you trying to look out for me, but I'm fine. Work comes first, and finding these kids remains at the top of my agenda."

"I'll bear that in mind, ma'am. Again, please accept my apologies."

The door opened behind Sara, and Carla tapped her on the shoulder.

"Morning. Did you get a good night's sleep?" were the first words out of her partner's mouth.

"I did, but I'm not liking what I've just been greeted with this morning."

Carla frowned. "Which is? No, don't tell me another child has gone missing?"

"All right, I won't, but I'd be frigging lying."

Jeff stood behind the counter, a sheepish expression distorting his features. "I should have rung you sooner."

"What's done is done, Jeff. Is this the parents' address?"

"Yes, the woman whose child has been abducted is called Yasmin Dickson, the top address is her own, and the bottom one is where she is at present, with her mother."

"Okay, we'll shoot over there. Will you inform the other team members to crack on with things in my absence?"

"Leave it with me, ma'am. Again, please accept my apologies, it won't happen again in the future."

Sara smiled. She struggled to be angry with someone who was only trying their best to care about her. "It's forgotten about, Jeff. Come on, Carla, we'll need to venture out early without added caffeine on hand to sustain us."

"In that case, we might need to stop off on the way. I

know what you're like first thing in the morning without a cup."

"That's charming. With friends like you…"

They jumped in the car, and Sara joined the traffic at the end of the road, which was barely moving faster than a tortoise on speed, this being the end of the rush hour. A couple of hundred yards, and the cars started flowing normally.

"How does that happen?"

Carla laughed. "I was thinking the same. It's a bloody miracle."

"One we should be grateful for, I suppose. How was your evening?"

"Peaceful. Des met up with a bunch of his mates, so I vegged out on the couch all night, dozed off a few times. You?"

"I curled up with Misty and Mark on the sofa. No idea what film we watched, my mind was too busy going over the case, and I couldn't be bothered watching it."

"I bet Mark was happy about that."

"He was fine. Left me to it. The film was more for men anyway."

"How did you sleep?"

"I got my full quota in, thank goodness."

Not long after, they drew up outside a small terraced house a few hundred feet from Asda.

"Apparently, she was walking along by the river behind the supermarket. Let's see what else she can tell us."

A patrol car passed by, and Sara waved.

The officer drew up and lowered his window. "Hello, ma'am, good to see you."

"Have you been searching the area for the missing child?"

"That's right. With little to go on, it's proving to be an impossible task."

"Keep doing it. We're heading in to have a word with the mother now."

"Good luck. We'll keep trawling the area until we're told otherwise."

"Let me know personally if you discover anything, if you would?"

"Of course." His window raised, and he drove off.

A young woman with red eyes and tear-stained, puffy cheeks opened the door to them.

Sara produced her warrant card. "Hello, is it Yasmin?"

The woman nodded and gestured for them to join her in the hallway.

"I'm DI Sara Ramsey, and this is DS Carla Jameson. I'm sorry you've been put in this position. I appreciate how difficult it must be for you at this time, but if you wouldn't mind going over the events leading up to your child being taken."

"Come in. I'm sorry, I'm feeling rather emotional and I'm likely to break down, so you'll have to forgive me."

"Nothing to forgive, I'd think badly of you if you didn't break down. I want to assure you that we have officers patrolling the streets as we speak. Hopefully, that will ease your mind a touch."

"It does, sort of. Come through, my mother is in the lounge."

"Oh, hello. Who are you?" Her mother shot out of the armchair close to the gas fire which was lit on a low flame.

Sara smiled and introduced herself and Carla a second time in as many minutes.

"I'm Afina. I'm so glad you're taking this seriously," she said with a slight accent.

"We are. I take it that you're aware of the other two cases of this nature that have already occurred this week?" Sara said.

"Yes, we've seen the news. That's why I contacted the

police right away," Yasmin stated. She sat on the arm of the chair her mother had returned to.

They grasped hands.

"You've definitely done the right thing. Is it all right if we take a seat?" Sara asked.

Yasmin thumped the side of her head. "Yes, please do. I'm sorry for my lack of manners."

Sara smiled and slid onto the brown leather sofa. Carla flipped open her notebook, ready for action.

"Where do I begin?" Yasmin asked. She pulled a tissue from the box and folded it on her lap.

"Perhaps you can tell us at what time the incident occurred?"

"I left home at seven. The sun was shining. It boosted my mood, and I wanted to get out of the flat."

"You need to tell them everything," Afina urged.

"Give me a chance, Mum. Don't interrupt my flow, you know my concentration levels are at their lowest at this time."

"I'm sorry, I'll keep my mouth shut," her mother said in a huff.

"Your mother is right, Yasmin, it would be better if you told us everything."

"I will, but in my own time. I left the flat and was strolling along the river. The bags were too heavy for the pram, and it tipped up. My fingers were trapped under the bar, and I didn't notice the person come up behind me. I've been so careful lately because of the news bulletins. I shouldn't have been out at that time of the morning, alone." Her head dipped, and she flattened out the creases in the tissue several times before she spoke again.

Sara allowed her the time to sort herself out.

Yasmin sucked in a breath and continued, "I walked out on my boyfriend. There was trouble between us last night. I decided to leave the flat at first light, or near enough while he was still in bed."

"So he didn't hear you leave the flat?"

"Not as far as I know. He's into drugs, you see. Once he's asleep, that's it. I decided it would be best for me and Jonas to leave him. Mum insisted on picking us up, but I didn't want her to, in case he woke up and kicked off." She cried and dabbed her eyes with the tissue. "I should have let her, at least then my baby would be here with us, safe. You have to help me. I can't stand the thought of him being harmed. He's such a good baby. Rarely cries, only when he's ill, and he's not been too good lately, he's had a chest infection. I shouldn't have taken him out that early. Why did I do that? Why?" Her voice broke on a heart-wrenching sob.

"It's okay. Try not to stress too much. You've given your son the best chance you could give him by getting in touch with us as soon as the incident happened."

"The officers who showed up were great. They insisted on taking me to hospital, but all I wanted to do was come home and be with Mum. She came to fetch me. That horrible person threw me in the river. It was so cold. I'm still shivering from the exposure now, either that or the shock is setting in. All I want to know is that my baby is safe. Is this about a ransom? Do you believe the same person you are after has taken my son?"

"Possibly. The other parents haven't received any ransom demands to date. At this moment, we're unsure what the perpetrator's motive is."

"But three babies? Or are there more that we don't know about yet?"

"Again, we don't know unless the parents come forward to inform us. I can't see any of them keeping that information from us. Therefore, I'm pretty confident that we're trying to find three babies. I have to ask the most obvious question here: do you believe your boyfriend could have anything to do with your child's abduction?"

The two women glanced at each other, their eyes widening as they processed the possibility.

It was Yasmin who broke eye contact with her mother and turned to face Sara. "No. He's done some pretty horrendous things to me over the years but he's never laid a hand on his son. I don't think he would have it in him to hurt Jonas."

"For all we know your baby hasn't been hurt, so maybe it's something we need to consider. Could he have been pretending to be asleep?"

"Maybe, but I genuinely believe he was asleep."

"What about friends and neighbours? Could one of them have alerted him to you moving out, possibly gone round there to wake him up?"

"I doubt it, he's not overly keen on the neighbours. He's given them all a mouthful here and there, and they've all turned their backs on him, on us, over the years."

"We'll drop round there and see him after we've finished here. Can you tell us more about the person who pushed you in the river? Was there only one person?"

"I think so. It all happened so quickly. I felt a light touch at first, and then someone pushed me towards the edge. Before I realised what was happening, I was there, teetering over the water, then the person gave me a final shove and I fell in. It was deeper than I anticipated it would be and I think I panicked. My own safety was at the forefront of my mind, and by the time I'd figured out what was going on, this person had taken the pram and was out of sight. They left the bags on the ground. A jogger was passing by afterwards. I cried out, and he pulled me out of the river. Luckily, I didn't put my phone in my pocket, I stored it in my bag last night. I was able to call my mother and then the police. Mum arrived first. She brought me a blanket; I was trembling, the water was so damn cold."

"I'm glad you're safe and that your personal ordeal was over and done with quickly. However, I'm truly sorry that your son is now missing. Anything you can tell us about this person is going to be a major help to our investigation. Did they talk to you? Do you know if the person concerned was male or female?"

"I didn't see them. They grunted in their effort to push me in the water. It sounded like a woman but I can't be one hundred percent sure."

"That's something. Did you catch what they were wearing at all?"

"Some kind of leisure suit and trainers. Wait, the trainers had stripes on them, if that helps?"

"Did the leisure suit have a hood?"

"Yes, yes it did. The hood was up, now that you've mentioned it. What else do I remember?" She shook her head. "No, there's nothing else."

"Okay, don't worry. I'll leave you my card, and if anything else comes to mind, you can ring me day or night to tell me. Which direction did they go, did you see?"

"They must have taken the shortcut through the Asda car park, at least I think they probably did." She broke down again.

Sara was concerned she was putting Yasmin under far too much pressure too soon. "Hey, you've done exceptionally well to come up with what you have. I'm not sure I would be able to do the same in your shoes."

Yasmin sniffled, and her mother slung an arm around her waist and rested her head against Yasmin's. "You're being so brave, my darling daughter. Listen to the police lady, she knows best. We'll get Jonas back before long, I have every confidence in the police. They're not like the police at home, they care about the general public here. At home they regard us as a hindrance."

"Where's home?" Sara asked, intrigued by the accent that had become further pronounced the more Afina spoke.

"We're from France but originally we came from Syria. We were refugees, and they treated us abysmally for years. I married a wonderful French man. He took a job in the UK, and we moved here over thirty years ago. I've tried to rid myself of my accent, but it still persists to linger and usually gets worse when I'm under stress or upset about something. Please, you have to help us. Don't let what I've told you about our heritage stop you from treating us like human beings."

Sara raised a hand. "I don't care about your past. We treat people as equals in this country, or should I say, my team does. We won't hold anything against you, you have my word."

"Thank you, that means a lot. Your officers who showed up to help my daughter were very good with us. They brought us back home, and the female officer even made us a drink."

"I'm glad to hear it. And your husband, where is he?"

A sad smile crossed her face. "Sadly, he passed away last year after a short illness. He caught Covid and was ill with that. It damaged his insides, and he struggled to fight off the lung infection he caught. He slipped away after a couple of days. A huge piece of my heart went with him. He was my guardian angel. Loved and cherished me like no other man throughout my life, and that includes my own father."

"That's right," Yasmin agreed. "We miss him every day. He saw us right when he left us, though, provided for Mum very well." A sadness descended over her once more. "I should have realised long ago that Ben wasn't a patch on my father. They despised each other, which didn't help. It wasn't until my father passed that Ben showed a different side to him. It's as though he was afraid to hit me while my father was alive in case Dad battered him. He's made up for it since."

"Have you reported the abuse to the police? Filed a complaint?"

Yasmin shrugged. "No, I didn't think there was any point. I've been saving up my money to leave him. I didn't want to burden Mum, and I intended to get a flat of my own at the end of next month, but things came to a head last night."

Sara inclined her head. "In what way, Yasmin?"

"He pulled a knife on me after I put Jonas to bed and... he..."

"Raped her. The fucking scum raped her," her mother shouted, tears streaming down her face.

"It's okay, Mumma, don't get upset. I need us both to be strong." Yasmin's gaze drifted back to Sara again. "I had to lie there all night beside him, the knife between us on the pillow. I was so tempted to use it on him but knew if I did, I could end my life in prison. No man is worth that, is he? I had Jonas to consider. That's why I left this morning. I had to, I couldn't take it any more." Another understandable sob broke out.

Sara's heart cracked a little over what the young mother had gone through in the last twenty-four hours. "I'm going to ask you to trust me. My team and I are working our socks off to find these children, and we will succeed. All I need from you is to have faith in us. If you think of anything else you can tell us in the meantime, reach out to me or the FLO when they arrive. Also, if the kidnapper gets in touch, again, ring me straight away."

"I will. You're my only hope to get my son back, I have no other option but to trust you."

"One last thing before we leave. I'm going to need a photo of the baby."

She showed her a picture of Jonas, and Sara agreed it was

just what they needed. "Send it to me, if you would? Right, if you'll allow us, we'd like to leave now and get the investigation underway. We're going to call at your flat, we have the address. How do you want us to play it with your, what shall we call him? Your ex-partner?"

"Definitely. He'll know that I've come here to Mum's. Is there anything you can do to keep him away from us?"

Sara winked and tapped the side of her nose. "You leave him to us, we're used to dealing with awkward customers, shall we say?"

Yasmin sighed and closed her eyes. "The last thing I need is him showing up here kicking off and making our lives a misery. Not that they can get any worse anyway."

"He won't come near you, don't worry."

Her eyes flickered open once more, and she squeezed her mother's shoulders. "I hope not. I'll show you to the door."

Afina gave her a relieved smile but remained seated.

Sara waved from the doorway and said, "Take care of yourself and each other."

"We will, providing you keep that vile man away from us."

"We're going to do our best." Sara closed the lounge door behind her and approached Yasmin and Carla. Lowering her voice, she said, "I know this is probably the last thing on your mind right now, but I really think you should consider bringing charges against your ex. He can't be allowed to get away with treating you like that."

"It's not the right time. All I want to do is forget about it, forget about him and his vile habit and lifestyle. What was I thinking, spending the past few years of my life with that disgusting animal?"

"They fool us into making us love them then invariably show their true colours," Carla said quietly. She touched Yasmin's arm and continued, "You're not the first woman to have the wool pulled over her eyes, and I doubt if you're going to be the last."

Yasmin clutched Carla's hand and asked, "Are you speaking from experience?"

Carla's gaze dropped to the doormat below her feet. "Women don't think twice about becoming one of these. We need to stand up for our rights to live *alongside* men in today's society, not be subservient to them. And yes, I speak from experience, therefore, I know what I'm talking about."

"Thank you for being so open with me. And are you with someone new who treats you well?"

"Yes, it didn't take me long to find the right man either. Let's worry about that side of things after we've got Jonas back with you. Planning for your future should be at the top of your agenda, once Jonas has been found."

"It will be, I promise. I have no intention of ever returning to that miserable existence ever again."

"Good. I can tell you're a strong woman. Hold on to that strength, and you'll soon turn your life around."

Sara was happy to take the back seat and allow Carla to issue her words of wisdom. She felt it was important for everyone in Yasmin's position to listen to someone who'd had the courage to break free from an abusive relationship. Their insight and courage were invaluable to an abused person. Then Carla surprised her a second time by hugging Yasmin and patting the young woman on the back.

"You've got this," Carla whispered.

Yasmin drew back, tears coursing down her cheeks. "Thank you, I believe I have. More importantly, I now believe in myself."

"And so you should," Carla said and smiled.

Carla left the house, and Sara had a quiet word of her own with Yasmin. "That was unexpected. Carla really went through the mill with her fella, suffered emotionally and physically, but like most women, she dug deep for her resolute streak to pull her through. We've all got one. I'm asking you to search for yours at this challenging time. I'll be in touch soon. Take care of yourself, Yasmin."

"Thank you, Inspector. I know I have the right team working on this investigation."

"You have. I've never intentionally let a member of the public down yet." Sara walked out of the house and back to the car where she found Carla sitting in the front seat and wearing a pensive expression.

Slipping behind the steering wheel, Sara asked, "Are you okay?"

"I am. Did I do the right thing, you know, telling her?"

"Only you can decide that, love. I think you did. You've successfully and indisputably turned your life around and come out the other side. That takes guts to achieve. Never forget that, or how far you've come in such a short time, partner."

"Mainly thanks to you, Sara. I'm going to be forever in your debt. If you hadn't intervened when you had, Lord knows what kind of emotional and physical mess I would be in by now."

"Nonsense. You'd already seen the light, you simply needed an extra nudge in the right direction, and the rest is history and should remain that way. Don't let it emerge again and cause doubts in your mind."

Carla shook her head. "As if I would."

"Yeah, as if you'd do such a thing, right? Anyway, you're going to need to rein in your feelings about this bastard because we're about to go and see him."

"I won't need an excuse to kick seven bells out of him if he tries it on with either of us."

Sara rolled her eyes and started the engine. "Hopefully, it won't come to that."

. . .

SHE WAS WRONG. Yasmin's former abusive, uptight boyfriend growled at them as soon as Sara produced her ID.

"Why the fuck are you two standing on my doorstep?" He greeted them dressed in grubby boxer shorts that had seen better days, his hair spiking in different directions, mimicking a porcupine, and smelling of a mixture of booze and drugs.

"Can we come in and discuss this?"

"No frigging copper is coming into my gaff uninvited. Say what you've got to say out here. It's all lies."

"What is?" Sara challenged.

"What she's told you. Yeah, I figured out she'd left me the minute I woke up. I don't give a shit about that but I refuse to allow her to make allegations that she can't back up."

"She's down at the station now, giving us DNA samples."

He tipped his head back and then straightened his face and glared at Sara. "You're dumber than you look if you think I'm gonna fucking fall for that one."

"Believe what you like. Anyway, that's not why we're here. We've come to see you about another matter. Any idea what that might be?"

"You think I'm some kind of Mystic Meg in my spare time? You're gonna need to tell me."

"Did you follow Yasmin when she left this morning?"

"Why would I want to do that? No, I was asleep in my pit. I reckon she must have drugged me last night, you know, put something in my beer to knock me out, so she could make her getaway with the kid in the morning. First I knew of it was when I woke up and her side of the bed was empty."

"But the knife was still in the same position, yes?" Sara asked, her eyes narrowing. He disgusted her. If Yasmin hadn't told her what he was like, just laying eyes on him for the first time would have given Sara the impression that Yasmin had delivered.

His lip curled up. "What knife?"

"The knife you held to her throat while you *raped* her last night?" Sara said, determined not to hold back.

His laugh echoed along the hallway of the flats and fell silent as quickly as it had appeared. "That's bullshit. You take her word for it and you're a bigger fool than you look."

"Is it? She showed us photographic evidence." Sara called his bluff, despite it being a lie.

"Again, that's utter bullshit. What's to stop her going into the kitchen, fetching a knife and putting it on the pillow between us?"

"How strange, that's the exact position Yasmin described."

"You told me a few minutes ago."

Sara turned to Carla and said, "Did I? I don't recall saying anything of the sort."

"That's because you didn't, Inspector," Carla confirmed.

Sara nodded and faced Abbott again. "I didn't think so."

"So arrest me for sleeping with a weapon under my pillow." He held out his hands and tapped his bare foot on the laminate flooring.

As tempted as Sara was to slap the cuffs on him, she restrained herself. "Funny that, you told us it was on the pillow a few seconds ago."

"On, under, what the fuck does it matter? I'm entitled to have it to hand, to protect myself. Have you any idea what a dangerous area this has become over the years? Filled with druggies and mini gangsters who think they're off the streets of New York."

"I had heard. Are you aware that if you attacked someone who entered your home with a knife, you'd be the one banged up for it, not them? Unless they used reasonable force, of course."

"Yeah, and that's what's frigging wrong with the law these days, innit?"

Sara chose to ignore the dig and instead challenged him further. "Where were you this morning?"

He glanced down at his boxer shorts and lily-white scrawny legs. "Doh, take a guess. Go on, you can do it. Or is it true what they say?"

Sara sighed. "And what's that?"

"That all women coppers have to do is flutter their eyelashes and show a bit of leg around the station to get a promotion these days."

Sara ignored the comment. "Have you left the flat this morning, yes or no?"

"It's pretty damned obvious what the answer is, well, maybe it would be to an officer with an ounce of intelligence."

"Get dressed."

He smirked and cocked an eyebrow. "What? You can't order me to do that."

"Can't I? Ben Abbott, I'm arresting you for perverting the course of justice. You do not have to say anything. But, it may harm your defence if you do not mention when questioned something which you later rely on in court. Anything you do say may be given in evidence."

"Fuck off, you can't do this."

"I can and I am. Sergeant, call for backup to join us."

Carla fished her phone out of her pocket and punched in the number for the station. She walked away to hold her conversation.

"This is bizarre. You can't do this." Abbott went to slam the door in their faces, but Sara stuck her foot in the way.

"We can and we will, unless you agree to cooperate with us."

He shrugged. "I have. I've told you what happened. If you

choose to believe her and your mind is made up, there's nothing I can do to change it, is there?"

"You can tell us if you've left the flat this morning, it's a simple sodding question."

"And I already answered it. Look at me, if I stepped onto the street dressed like this, I'd get done by your lot for flashing, wouldn't I?"

Sara sighed and decided to press on, what with time not being on their side. "Okay. Now that you've calmed down a bit, I can reveal the truth behind our visit here today."

His brow pinched into a deep frown. "Meaning?"

"Meaning, that yes, Yasmin left you today, and I'm led to believe with good reason, but that's beside the point. Whilst she was walking, laden down with her bags and the pram, she was attacked and thrown into the river."

His head jutted forward, and he ran his hand through his already spiky hair. "You what? Is she okay? Is she in hospital? Should I go and see her?"

Sara wagged her finger. "I'm not telling you this so that your conscience is pricked enough to want to visit her, I can guarantee that's the last thing she'd want at this time. I'm obliged to tell you that during the incident, your son was abducted."

He fell silent for a second or two then clenched his fist and lashed out at the front door. It swung back and forth and bit back a few times, bashing against his elbow when he least expected it. "My son has been taken, and you're standing on my doorstep having a pop at me. What the fuck? What are you doing about it? You should be out there, searching the streets for him. How far could they have got?"

Sara shrugged. "If you've listened to the news at all this week, you'll have heard that this is the third baby who has been kidnapped in the past few days."

He ran his hand through his hair again. "What the fuck

are you useless bitches doing about it? I demand to speak to your superior officer. Is it a man or woman?"

"She's a woman. That's your prerogative, but she won't tell you any differently to what I'm telling you. We have officers out there, hunting high and low for the children."

"That figures. You women are getting everywhere."

"That's a pretty offensive comment to say, and I have to advise you that you're not doing yourself any favours in the eyes of the law, blatantly showing your dislike for women."

"So, arrest me. Add another charge to the one you're trying to hit me with already. You're the ones who are going to end up with egg dripping off your faces."

"Can we cut the crap?" Sara said. "What we need to know is if you can think of anyone who would want to abduct your son."

"Simple answer to that, no. Next question? Bearing in mind that you're wasting time standing on my doorstep, hounding me while some fucking no-mark has kidnapped my skin and blood. Show some urgency, for fuck's sake. Get on with it and get out there to search for him. Jesus, if you lot had brains, you'd be fucking unbelievably dangerous, and the criminals wouldn't stand a frigging chance. It's a shame we haven't reached that stage yet."

"All this isn't doing you any good, Mr Abbott. Often when people become instantly defensive, it's generally because they have something to hide. Have you?"

"Bollocks! No, I ain't."

Carla rejoined the conversation. "They're on their way."

"Oh good. I'd better dust off my boxing gloves in that case." Abbott smirked.

"From what I hear, you're pretty useful with your hands, with or without gloves on."

"Listening to that bitch again? You should know better

than to do that, Inspector. Women are known stretchers of the truth."

Sara raised an eyebrow and cocked her ear. Sirens sounded in the distance. "You've got two minutes to make yourself look presentable."

"And if I refuse?"

"Then you'll be taken in by force. The way you've treated and spoken to us since our arrival leads me to believe that you're hiding the truth from us, Abbott."

"You'll be telling me next you can read me like a book."

"It goes with the territory. Now, are you going to cooperate with us or not? The choice is yours."

The sirens edged ever closer. Sara could see the conflict in his eyes.

He shrugged. "Tell me what you want from me."

"I want to know if you've done anything dodgy lately, either to do with drugs or not, that could possibly have put your child in danger."

"And I'm telling you for the second or third time, is it now? No, there is nothing. Yes, I take drugs but I do it on the sly, if you like. I can do without them, unlike some folks I know."

"Is that true?" Sara said, an edge of disbelief to her tone.

"Yes, they don't rule my life, and if that bitch has told you differently, then she's lying."

"Perhaps you'd care to tell us why you aren't at work then?"

"Nope, I shouldn't have to. Fuck, all right then, it's my week off. I bet the bitch didn't tell you that, did she?"

"And you work where?"

"I've got a stall with a friend on the markets. We travel around the county most days."

"Selling what?"

"Trainers mostly. Why?"

"Just getting the facts down, that's all."

Two officers appeared in the stairwell, and Abbott got fidgety.

"You can call off the hounds. I ain't done nothing wrong."

"Haven't you? I beg to differ, but we're going to give you the benefit of the doubt this time, in light of the circumstances."

"You mean because my kid is missing and all you're doing is bloody making a nuisance of yourself on my doorstep."

Sara raised an eyebrow. "We'll leave it there, for now. A word of caution for you."

"Here goes, what's that?"

"Keep away from Yasmin."

"Try and keep me away from her, the silly bitch has just lost my frigging kid."

"If necessary, we'll offer the advice she needs to keep herself safe." Sara turned and walked away.

"Yeah, and I'll make sure my solicitor makes your life hell, Inspector."

"Enough of the threats," the older male officer shouted.

Carla caught up with Sara and tugged on her arm. "Hang on, I thought you were going to arrest him?"

"I was but then thought better of it. You saw how feisty he was. Can you imagine how miserable he's likely to make Yasmin's life if we pursue it further?"

"Even more miserable than she's led over the past few years? Come on, Sara, this isn't like you to back down when pressed. Why now? Why with that moron?"

"Something is telling me to back off, Carla. I'm listening to my gut on this one."

Carla shook her head, apparently bamboozled by her excuse. "I'm just putting this out there. In this instance, I think you're wrong. That scumbag needs hauling over a twenty-foot run of hot coals."

"In your unbiased opinion, is that what you're saying?"

Carla continued walking, and Sara trotted to catch her up at the top of the steps that would lead them down to the car.

"Don't walk off in a huff. If you've got something to say, then say it."

"I've said all that needs to be said. We're on different pages, and I think it would be better if we let this conversation end here."

"You're pissed at me because I didn't arrest him for the rape. Think about it, Carla, I couldn't do that, not until Yasmin raises a complaint against him. Maybe she'll do that after her child has been found, but right now, her main priority lies with her son, and that should go for us, too. The rape allegation can be dealt with in the future, if she wishes to pursue it. That decision is out of our hands. You must realise that, Carla."

Carla sighed and glanced out at the River Wye, winding its way through the city in the distance. "I still think he got off lightly back there. You could have been more forceful with him. What if he's behind the kidnappings?"

"After speaking with him, I seriously doubt he would have the brains for carrying out anything so underhand, do you?"

"He's into drugs. Have you forgotten about the lies your brother told you in order to get funds for his next snort?"

"No, I haven't, and thank you for reminding me, even if it was below the belt."

"Sorry, I didn't mean it to be. Which is why I think we should draw a line under this now and move on before either one of us says something we will regret."

"Again," Sara added.

The two officers caught up with them at the top of the stairs.

"I take it we're no longer needed, ma'am?" the older one asked.

"That's right. Sorry to have wasted your time. There was a minute or two back there where we thought he might kick off. I wanted to be prepared."

"Happy to oblige, you know that, ma'am. Enjoy the rest of your day."

"Thanks."

Sara watched the two officers run down the stairs in front of them. "I can't see us having a nice day, can you?"

Carla shrugged. "It hasn't started out too well. I can't see that changing anytime soon."

CHAPTER 7

*S*ara felt the need to call another press conference to keep the investigation in the eye of the public. Jane managed to action one within an hour of Sara asking. The same obnoxious journalist had it in for Sara but, thanks to Jane's wise words before she stepped onto the stage, she managed to combat all his awkward questions with poise, in the process wiping the smug smile off his face.

That evening, Craig and Barry both agreed to remain behind to answer any likely calls that might come their way. Exhausted, Sara drove home to spend the evening with Mark and Misty. Even though her mind was elsewhere for most of it, they enjoyed a nice meal and watched a new film available on Netflix. At the end of it, Sara regretted her wasted evening, not for the first time, with that channel.

"Why do we bloody bother with it?" she complained.

Mark laughed. "You forgot the twenty minutes rule."

She cringed. "I did. Sorry, I was a little distracted. It was around that time that I mentally switched off from it and spent the rest of the film going over the investigation in my mind."

"Don't think I hadn't noticed. If you'd given the film a chance, it turned out to be a decent plotline, come the end."

She rose from her seat and collected their empty wine glasses. "Glad you enjoyed it. I'm off to bed. Do you want anything else before I go up?"

"I'll join you. You see to Misty's needs while I finish putting the dishes away. I left them on the side because you were eager to watch the film."

Sara poked her tongue out at him and got on with her chores. After letting Misty in from the garden, she noticed her phone vibrating across the kitchen table. "I'm going to have to get this for obvious reasons," she said, by way of an apology.

"Go ahead. I'd rather you answer it now than when we're having a cuddle in bed."

Sara smiled and jabbed the button on her phone to accept the call. "DI Sara Ramsey."

"Sorry to disturb you, ma'am, it's Barry here."

"Don't worry, Barry. What have you got for me?"

"We received a call a few minutes ago from a woman who possibly witnessed the abduction that happened this morning."

"Tell me more."

"She said she saw a woman pushing the pram away from the river, across the supermarket car park. She thought it was strange as the woman kept peering over her shoulder. She presumed that someone must have been following her, judging by her reaction, but the caller didn't see anyone suspicious hanging around, otherwise she would have called the police."

"Excellent news, although I bet the caller feels devastated she didn't intervene now."

"She does. I tried to reassure her, but she was having none

149

of it. She's got children of her own and struggled to compre-
hend what it must feel like to have one kidnapped."

"I'm sure. Did she say anything else? Did the woman get
in a car?"

"Not that she could tell. We can get onto Asda's in the
morning, see what footage they can offer us. Past experience tells me it's a waste of time ringing at this time of
night."

"That's a good call, Barry. Anything else come in this
evening?"

"Nothing, other than a few abusive calls about us not
taking our job seriously enough to capture this dickhead. I
know they're talking out of their arses, but it still feels like
someone plunging the knife in. What do they think we do all
day long, sit at our desks making paper planes?"

"It's best if you ignore people like that, love. We know
differently, that's all that counts. Go home, get some rest,
you've done more than your fair share today."

"Thanks, boss. I can't believe how little we're getting from
these conferences."

"I can't either, that's what makes all this so frustrating. All
we need is that one phone call, but it's like extracting hen's
teeth. Hopefully, tomorrow will be a brighter and more positive day. Thanks for agreeing to stay behind. Pass on my
appreciation to Craig as well. I'll see you both bright and
early in the morning."

"I will, boss. Enjoy the rest of your evening."

"Thanks, you, too." Sara ended the call and closed her
eyes, disappointed that the appeal hadn't produced more, yet
again.

*What is it going to take for the public to appreciate how serious
this situation is? Without their help, we're screwed, well and truly.*

Mark laid his hands on her shoulders and massaged the
knots deep within her muscles that unbeknownst to her

were crying out for his touch. "Are you all right? Was it bad news?"

"No, it was the opposite. Although, I doubt it's going to lead us anywhere. That feels good, thank you."

"It would be better if it were skin on skin. Come on, let's get to bed, and I'll show you what I mean."

Sara stood and kissed him.

THE BABIES WERE HARDER to deal with than she'd ever anticipated. "What the fuck? If I change one more shitty nappy, it'll be too soon. It's like painting the Forth Bridge. No sooner have I come to the end than I have to start over again." Her mobile rang, mid-nappy change on Jonas. "Stay there, don't move or you'll get some of this." She held her clenched fist against the screaming boy's face. He'd been crying and screaming intermittently since she'd taken him that morning. "Bloody nuisance. Still, that's boys for you, always needing their mummies!"

She left the room and answered her call from her contact. "Hi, I was going to give you a ring later to see how things are going."

"Fine at this end. You?"

"Not really. I've got three ankle-biters here now, one more to get, and that's my job complete. It's been tougher than I thought."

"In what way? You've certainly been attracting attention through the news, which, may I remind you, wasn't part of the bargain."

"Meaning what?"

"Meaning that my clients are getting their knickers in a bloody twist."

"Tough. What did they expect? Kids would go missing and the police would just shrug their shoulders and do nothing about it? Hardly, they need to come down to the real world. In fact, all this shit I'm dealing with, literally, has just bumped my prices up."

"What? You can't do that."

"Can't I? Sue me. Oh no, that's right, you can't, because all this is dodgy, ain't it?"

"We had a deal. You can't go back on it now. I've got families getting ready to accept the kids, to welcome them into their homes, and here you are, pulling this frigging stunt on me."

"So what's the alternative? Pay up or what?"

"Jesus, you're one twisted fucker. I should never have got into bed with you."

"I'll push that disgusting thought to one side, if you don't mind. I prefer a man between my legs, not a woman."

"I'm not one of those."

"You really want to continue with this conversation? I have more important things to do, like searching for a different contact to take these sprogs off my hands, if you're going to dig your heels in about stumping up with the cash."

"I'll need time to gather the funds together."

"I'm due to make the drop-off in forty-eight hours. I'll give you twenty-four to get the funds deposited into my account or don't bother contacting me again."

"We've got a contract. You can't negate on it now."

"Get the cash or I walk, it's as simple as that."

"And what about the kids? I'm the one who has a list of contacts, that's the reason you came to me in the first place."

"You can be replaced. I'll send them abroad if I have to, just to get rid of them."

"*You can't do that.* I've got families expecting the kids to join them this week. I wouldn't want to get on the wrong side of some of these people either. Come on, Fiona, give me a break."

"I will, after I see the extra money in my account by five o'clock tomorrow, got that?" She ended the call and stuck her two fingers up at the phone. "Take that, bitch. It's your fault for doing deals with the devil. There was only ever going to be one winner." She laughed and then returned to her nappy-changing duties. This time she added a peg to her nose to combat the smell that had emerged in her absence.

"You filthy little fucker." Thoughts of rubbing the little brat's nose in the mess he'd made streaked through her mind, but it didn't manifest into anything else.

Tasks completed, she switched off the light, hoping the kids' crying would die down and they would finally drop off to sleep. Panic mode set in when she sat down with a glass of wine and recapped the conversation she'd had with Liz. What was she thinking? Making threats that she knew she couldn't fulfil. If Liz dropped out now, what the fuck was she supposed to do with the babies? Liz was right, they needed each other, and pulling that stunt had probably screwed up the deal. Greed had played a part in that exercise.

She finished her drink and then went to bed. That was until the babies started crying, one after the other. Sleep deprivation, she'd never known it had existed until this gig.

Why the effing hell do people choose to give life to a crying, pooing little human who does its best to ignore all the threats under the sun and continue to do what it sodding well likes?

Dead on her feet, she collapsed into bed an hour later after the kids had finally worn themselves out. She crossed her fingers, hoping the long-awaited reprieve would last.

A NOISE DISTURBED her a few hours later. She removed the knife from under her pillow, pulled on her trousers and crept down the stairs. She froze as a figure appeared in front of her. This could only mean one thing... she turned to run.

The person latched on to her ankle and yanked her down the stairs. Her grip tightened around the knife, and she swung it back and forth, not caring if she did any damage to her attacker or not.

He cried out and staggered backwards. Another figure came rushing at her. The knife took on a life of its own in her attempt to escape the other man. He hadn't bothered wearing a mask, like the other one. Why not? Had they presumed that she wouldn't put up a fight? They were wrong. She fought like a lioness protecting her cubs.

"Why, you fucking whore. Put the goddamn knife down or I swear to God I'm going to kill you."

"You're going to do that anyway, right?"

"No. That wasn't the intention. The boss sent us here to collect the kids. You've overstepped the mark, shit for brains."

"Ha, and she hasn't, relying on you two louts to take me on?"

She jabbed forward, and the knife caught him in the side. He grunted and toppled to the right, shocked. But that only seemed to infuriate him more, and after a moment's pause he surged forward, his focus on relieving her of the weapon. She could tell the wound was hampering his progress, and she kept going for him with short, sharp movements.

He yelled as the knife struck its target.

"Go, before you end up like your partner in crime, dead."

"Fucking bitch. You ain't seen the last of me."

Fiona mimicked him and said, "Ooo... get you, I'm shaking in my size six boots."

He gave her the finger and hoisted his mate's body over his shoulder, grunting as the weight affected his legs.

"Fuck off and don't come back. You won't get out of here alive next time. And tell that bitch of a boss to do one. The deal is off. I'll get rid of the kids myself, it's no biggie."

"Yeah, right. So you think. Good luck with that one. You're deluded if you think you can palm them off onto anyone else after being all over the news."

His words ran through her mind as she secured the house. She placed a kitchen chair under the back door handle, something she should have thought about doing before when she'd gone to bed. She felt trapped. She had nowhere else to go and now considered herself a sitting duck. If Liz had sent two guys already, what was to stop her sending more? All she could do was secure the place as tightly as possible in the hope they gave up.

What the fuck am I going to do? How can I get rid of the kids? I'm out of pocket by nearly a grand already, so killing them isn't an option.

She spent the rest of the night camped out in the lounge with a selection of knives by her side. Thankfully, no further incidents occurred that night, but it didn't stop her feeling on edge. She'd sent Liz a message to say the money she wanted had now increased to ten grand, but the woman hadn't replied to the request. Fiona kicked herself for blotting her copy book.

CHAPTER 8

Sara and Carla had not long returned from having a chat with the manager of Asda, who had willingly given them the footage from the previous day. Now that they had a genuine lead to follow up on, Sara thought their lives were about to get easier. She handed the disc to Craig to work his magic and, to everyone's relief, he successfully manipulated the image into something they could work with.

Sara was the first to congratulate him. "I'm going to get onto Forensics, something I should have chased up yesterday. See what they have for us." She raced into her office and picked up her landline.

The technician was apologetic when she finally traced him. "Sorry, I knew there was something I should have done yesterday before I left. I'll send over the image that I managed to enhance for you."

"Thanks, not to worry. We all get days when we're overwhelmed with work."

"You're not wrong. The workload is massive around here

at present. Thanks for being so understanding, Inspector. I'm hitting the Send button as we speak."

Sara started up her computer and urged it to hurry up. Finally, her emails popped up, and the one from the lab was right at the top. She opened it to have a look at the image that was still very grainy to her eyes. "Is there any chance you can put a copy in the post for me?"

"I'll do it now before I forget again."

"Thanks. Great work, don't worry about the delay." She tried to hide her disappointment and ended the call. Ignoring the heaving in-tray she hadn't got around to touching in days, she printed off a copy and left her office again, handed Craig the image. He blew up the other photo they had been working with, that of the woman from the supermarket car park, and between them, they took a punt that it was probably the same woman. Sara stared at the picture over and over, holding the one that had come through from the lab at different angles until the penny dropped.

Shocked, she perched on the desk beside Craig. "Shit!"

"Hey, boss. You look like you've seen a ghost, what's going on?"

"It's her," Sara mumbled.

"Sorry, who is she?"

Carla joined them and removed the image from Sara's hand. "Who is it? You're worrying us now, Sara, who the heck is it?"

"The woman who witnessed the first baby being snatched outside Aylestone Park. What was her name? Damn." She glanced at the whiteboard, and her gaze fixed on Mandy Fuller's name. She pointed at the board. "The bloody first witness I spoke to. She fed me a bunch of lies to cover her tracks. And I sodding well believed her."

"Don't be hard on yourself, you couldn't have known she was the one, not if she was that convincing," Carla said.

Sara gasped, the realisation dawning. "I've got her name. She should be easy to trace."

Carla cocked an eyebrow. "Worth a shot. However, she probably supplied you with a fake one. Sounds like she's a cunning bitch, probably wouldn't be foolish enough to give you her proper name, would she?"

"I guess. Let's do the necessary searches, just in case. I'm going to run something past Jane. I'll be back in a tick." She trotted into the office and closed the door behind her, pausing only briefly to cast her eye out of the window and take in her favourite view to calm her racing heart. "Jane, it's me again, pest. I need to run something past you, get your opinion on a certain issue that has cropped up."

"Okay, I'm intrigued. What's wrong?"

"I've been duped and think I need to call someone out on TV."

"Duped? How?"

"The first baby who was abducted, do you remember me telling you that a witness came forward and told me that she saw a man bundling the baby into the car?"

"I do. What's the problem, Sara?"

"I believe she's the bloody kidnapper. She came out into the open to intentionally drive the investigation in the wrong direction."

Jane gasped. "Oh no, that's despicable. What a callous, evil thing to do."

"Yeah, she definitely has an evil intent, I'll give her that. We're just delving into the details she gave us now. I'm presuming she furnished us with a fake identity and address."

"And you need to call another press conference to see if anyone knows her, is that it?"

"I was hoping you would agree. I know it's asking a lot, this will be our fourth conference this week, it might come across as desperation."

"You are, *desperate* to find the babies. I've got no objection asking the journalists to come in again. It shows you care about what happens to the little ones and that you're doing your utmost to get them back."

"You're amazing. And here I was, sitting here dreading that you might knock me back, possibly regard it as overkill."

"Not at all. That's what I'm here for. Let me try and get this organised for you this morning, how would that be?"

"Fabulous, if you can pull it off. Thanks, Jane, as always."

"Don't thank me too soon."

Sara hung up and sat back in her chair. Mandy Fuller's image haunted her thoughts. *You evil, conniving, bitch. I'm going to have your arse for this.* She leapt out of her chair and returned to the incident room.

"Okay, let's gather all the footage together, from every scene, and go over it until something comes to light that we can act upon."

Craig and Barry leapt into action.

"Bring up all the relevant points that have been raised so far on the big screen, Craig. I'm particularly interested in the car at the pharmacy. We've got a reasonable image of the woman, let's concentrate on her car. Shit, I'll be right back." She picked up the nearest phone and rang the front desk. "Jeff, I need you to do me a huge favour."

"Name it, ma'am."

"The woman who came in earlier this week, I think it was on Monday, but I can't be sure, my mind feels like a tornado has taken root and is swirling in a vast vortex. She was called Mandy Fuller."

"I recall the woman, and yes, I believe it was Monday, the day that baby was kidnapped outside the park."

"That's right. You're never going to believe this, but I think she's the kidnapper."

"What! You're kidding me, no, scrap that, you wouldn't be as cruel as to do that, would you?"

"No, I wouldn't. She's played us, came in here with some cock-and-bull story and led us a bloody merry dance, all the while laughing at us. I feel sick to the stomach."

"I'm not surprised. What can I do for you?"

"Can you get me a clear image of her from the camera at the front door? It's pretty urgent. I've got pictures of her at a couple of the crime scenes, but the images are either grainy or only showing half of her face, nothing that we can call definitive. If you can supply me with a clear image, I have Jane arranging yet another press conference for me. I can air it in an appeal, see if that'll flush her out."

He sucked in a breath. "Risky, ma'am, if you don't mind me saying."

"I don't, and I know you're right, but what's the alternative? There isn't one. We've been working this investigation all week, and she's gone out of her way to make sure she put us off the scent and on the wrong route, intentionally hampering our progress."

"What if she flips and decides to get rid of the kids?" Jeff countered.

"Don't worry, the thought has already crossed my mind. Hopefully, plastering her face all over the news will give us all the ammunition we need to bring her down. It's going to block any move she is intending to make, at least that's the plan. We have no idea what her motive is. What she's proposing to do with the babies, or whether she's still got them. If we sit around doing sod all then she's continuing to get one over on us, isn't she?"

"I get the dilemma, ma'am. Let me see what I can do. Once I have the image for you, I'll send it up and at the same time get it distributed to the troops."

"I was about to suggest the same. Thanks, Jeff."

She ended the call to find Carla standing beside her with a coffee.

"One thing you forgot to ask Jeff."

Sara frowned. "What was that?"

"If he could search the car park for her vehicle."

"Good call. I'll run it past him. Let's get a clear picture of her first. Thanks for the drink, I needed this. I have a good feeling this is all coming together at the right time."

"We'll see. I wouldn't get my hopes up too soon. We've still got to rescue the babies. What if she's dumped them? Stolen them to sell and has given them away within hours of abducting them?"

"We won't know the answers to either of those questions until we find her, Carla. First things first, eh? This remains our priority, locating that bitch and her bloody car."

THE MORNING WHIZZED PAST. Jane accomplished what she set out to achieve, and the conference took place at eleven-thirty that morning. The journalists all seemed pretty pissed off to be summoned yet again, but Sara was past caring. Why should she? She had more important issues to worry about, like finding the babies before something sinister happened to them. Knowing what a callous and evil woman they were dealing with now only succeeded in making Sara's anxiety levels escalate.

"This is the person of interest I was referring to. The name she has given us, Mandy Fuller, is probably a fake name. Do you know this person? Has anyone out there had any dealings with her over the years? Has she worked for you? Have you seen her around your neighbourhood? Shop-keepers, has she visited your shop for supplies? Pub land-lords or managers, has she frequented your premises during the past few weeks? Someone must recognise her. Please come forward if you do. Call the number at the bottom of your screen for the sake of these children. Dig deep, and please tell us if you've had any sort of connection with this woman in the past."

Jane called the conference to a halt before Sara got bombarded by fierce questions from certain parties in the room, namely the obnoxious journalist, with whom Sara had deliberately avoided eye contact throughout the appeal. Outside, in the anteroom, Sara decompressed and shook her arms out.

"We did it. Thanks to you, Jane. Let's hope something comes of the plea this time. I'm not sure what we're going to do if we draw a blank again. We've never had such a lack-lustre response from the public before, or if we have, I can't remember."

"Yeah, that's the main concern I have that we're not reaching the right people with these conferences."

"Why is that? The investigation involves kids being abducted. Are we to believe that people just don't care these days? Are they too scared to get in touch in case we suspect them of being involved?"

Jane pointed and nodded at Sara. "I think you've hit the nail on the head. Perhaps the general public are too fright-ened to get in touch."

"Jesus, this is what's wrong with our world these days, people are too reserved or maybe too confused."

"Yep, I said the same thing to my dad only last week. He was a community bobby, out there, walking the streets most days, rain or shine. The people in the neighbourhood he covered trusted him, knew they could rely on him to watch out for and reprimand their kids if it was necessary. There's nothing of that ilk today, sadly."

"I didn't know your father was a police officer. I can see

why you're such a professional now. Did you have any thoughts about joining up?"

"No, it never crossed my mind, although I do love working for the police in my role. Behind the scenes instead of being thrust out there, into the limelight, is a dream come true for me."

"I understand, being on the frontline isn't for everyone. Right, I suppose I'd better prepare the troops in case we're inundated with calls."

"Let's hope putting a face to the perpetrator will prick the public's consciences and you get an instant result from it."

"We've done our best. That's all we can do and hope it pays off. Hopefully, this will be the last conference we have to put out there to do with this investigation. It's getting a tad tedious, even for me."

"I see it as a means to an end. Showering the public with facts can only be a good thing. Like you stated during the conference, someone out there must know this woman. The sooner they come forward, the sooner the bitch will be behind bars. Sorry, I don't often swear, but you're not the only one worked up about this case."

"Yeah, I think it's getting to us all. Let's face it, we'd have to be cold-hearted for it not to."

"True enough. Speak to you soon. Ring me if I can be of further assistance, Sara."

"Your name will be at the top of my list."

Sara returned to the incident room. Actually, she didn't, not straight away. Instead, she turned right at the top of the stairs and decided it would be a good time to bring DCI Price up to date with their progress. Price was a little surprised that Sara didn't have better news for her, which only made Sara feel worse. She trudged back to the incident room and went directly to her office. That's where Carla found her a few minutes later, with her head in her hands.

"What's happened?"

"Nothing, as far as I know. That's the problem. Price has just read me the riot act, had the audacity to ask me if I had pulled out all the stops on this case or if I was leaving some in reserve to use later."

"The bloody nerve of that woman, she knows full well you wouldn't do that. I hope you put her straight?"

Sara glanced up and shrugged. "I didn't have it in me to do it."

"What? So you sat there while she tore you to shreds?"

"Neither, even though it's true."

Carla slumped into the chair. "Fuck, you can't let her get to you."

"Why not? She's not saying anything I haven't said internally to myself."

"Christ on a beach ball, have you listened to yourself? How the hell is that attitude going to help us solve this case? We're all aware how frustrating it is and how much our backs are against the wall, but dwelling on it is only going to stamp all over the good stuff we have in our favour."

"Name me two things, I dare you!"

"Bloody hell, I've never heard the like. You've identified the perpetrator, that's got to be right up there."

"I said two things."

Carla paused and seemed pensive. "All right, you've got me by the short and curlies. You can't let the boss grind you down like this. Is she aware of how many press conferences you've put yourself through this week?"

Sara nodded. "I told her. She said that was two too many and advised me not to hold any more, if only to save face."

"I can't believe she said that. And there was me thinking how cool she was and totally different to other DCIs I've heard about in the past."

"Well, there you have it. In a way, she's right. I don't really mind her having a go at me when it's justified. I'll carry on and suffer in silence. Let her believe she's won this round, when she clearly hasn't. We're all aware of how much we've been up against it on this investigation. Unless you're in the thick of it, I suppose from an outsider's point of view, it must seem we've been dragging our feet over this one."

"Which couldn't be further from the truth. Maybe she should get her fat arse out of that chair from time to time and come down to the real world."

"Oh, I should, should I?" a stern voice said from behind.

Sara and Carla stared at each other for a few seconds until Sara cleared her throat and raised her hand in objection.

"Carla didn't mean anything by that, DCI Price."

"Didn't she? Then why say it? No, don't bother replying, Carla is right. I've come down here to apologise to you, Sara, you didn't deserve me speaking to you that way. I know you and your team always give each and every case one hundred percent effort. I'd just received a call from the care home about a family member who has taken a fall. My behaviour was unacceptable. I must dash. I need to inform the rest of the family who bother to visit my Aunt Maisy. They reckon the fall was bad enough to warrant an extra stay in hospital."

"Ouch, sounds nasty. We all have personal issues we need to combat now and again, boss."

"We do, but that will never excuse the way I spoke to you."

Sara smiled, and the nerves twisting her insides faded when Price left the room.

Carla covered her face with her hands and shook her head. "Fuck, fuck, fuck. Why did I have to put both sodding feet in my mouth at such an inappropriate time?"

"Shit happens," Sara said. "Come on, let's join the others, I think I heard the phones ringing out there."

"It could be wishful thinking on your part."

"Probably."

They left the room to see if Sara was right. She was, and the team announced they'd had a small flurry of calls come in during the last thirty minutes. There were a few cranks amongst them that the team had so far managed to dismiss.

"This one is interesting, boss." Jill held up a sheet of paper. "The caller, Kittie Jackson, said she used to work with a woman who looked like Mandy Fuller, except she recalls her name being either Fiona or Felicity, she couldn't remember which."

"Interesting. Did she hint at a surname for this mystery woman?"

"No, she didn't. She gave me the contact details of her former employer. Do you want me to give them a call, see if they can supply us with her full name?"

"Great idea, thanks, Jill."

Sara moved around the room. "I know I keep hounding you about the car, guys," she said to Craig and Barry. "But you can see how imperative it is for us to find the vehicle before it's too late."

"It might be that already," Barry grumbled. "For all we know, she might be stealing cars, using them to carry out the abductions, and then dumping them. She's obviously shrewd, otherwise she wouldn't have the nous to distort her number plate."

"Fair point. Keep searching. As soon as we get her name verified, then I sense there will be no stopping us. Until such a time, we need to press on with every avenue open to us."

"We're on it, boss," Barry replied, his gaze focused on his computer screen.

"I've got it!" Jill shouted.

Her triumphant cry startled Sara, and she raced towards Jill's desk.

"You have? What is it?"

"Fiona Lyle. I'm going to run it through the system, see if she's known to us."

"You do that, thanks, Jill. Craig, get in touch with DVLA, see if they'll supply her reg number and make of car, you never know your luck. I'm sure you'll be able to work your charm on them."

"I'm glad you have faith in my abilities, boss." He smiled and picked up the phone on his desk to make the call.

The phone rang again, this time on Christine's desk. She answered it, and Sara inched towards her and peered over her shoulder at the notes Christine was jotting down. It was an address. Sara's heart lifted, her expectation brimming over.

"A neighbour has given me her address and said that she's seen Lyle take a couple of children, or babes in arms, as she put it, into the house over the past few days. She didn't think anything of it at the time, thought Lyle had changed her job again and become some kind of child minder. It wasn't until she saw Fiona's photo on the screen that things slotted into place. Now she's kicking herself for not getting in touch with us sooner."

"At least she's rectified that now. Did she say if Fiona is still there? Has she seen her lately?"

"She didn't say."

"Okay. Carla, you and I need to get over there ASAP."

"Want us to join you, boss?" Barry shouted.

"Yes, sounds like a plan. Craig, have you got through to DVLA yet?"

"Not yet, I'm on ruddy hold."

"Not to worry. Marissa, would you kindly take over? We've got her address now, all we're missing is the make and model of the car. While you're waiting for them to answer, place a call to the front desk, chase Jeff up for me. He was supposed to be trawling through the footage around the time

Fiona visited me on Monday. Dropping him a reminder wouldn't go amiss."

"On it now, boss."

SARA, Carla, Barry and Craig tore down the stairs. Sara ensured she and Craig signed out a couple of Tasers on the way out to the cars. Fiona Lyle's address turned out to be a stone's throw from the station. Sara wondered if Lyle had maybe walked to the station at the beginning of the week, which would account for Jeff not getting back to her regarding the car.

Sara led the way and parked up a fair distance from the house they needed and then gestured for her two colleagues to join them. Craig and Barry jumped in the back, and they went over a plan that Sara had contemplated during the drive to the location.

"Carla, you and Craig ease around to the rear of the property while Barry and I take the front door. Keep your eyes open, call me if you see anything happen, and for goodness' sake, keep an eye out for the babies. Craig, don't make any rash moves regarding the Taser, let's see how things pan out first. Anyone got any questions?"

"What if she tries to harm the babies as soon as she sees us?" Craig asked.

"Then you have my permission to warn her, and if she chooses to ignore it, don't be afraid to take aim—obviously avoid hurting the babies. Knowing how devious she is, I wouldn't put it past her to try and use them as a human shield. I want you to be prepared for that if she does."

Sara watched Carla and Craig make their way up a side alley around the back of the row of terraced houses. Lyle's was in the middle.

"Can you see any movement inside, either upstairs or down?" Sara asked Barry.

"Nothing. All seems too quiet to me."

"I wish we had the heads-up on what car she drives."

"Yeah, that's a huge negative for us."

Sara opened her car door. "Let's make a move, the others should be in position by now."

"Want me to give Craig a call to find out?"

"Has he switched his phone over to vibrate?" Sara knew what the answer would be before Barry gave it.

"Always when he's out in the field. He loves it, being out here in the thick of things as opposed to sitting behind a desk, banging his head against it most of the time."

Sara smirked. They waited another moment or two until the response came back. "I bet. Right, they're in position, so here we go."

They approached the house, cautiously, keeping out of sight of the front windows. The closer they got, the heavier the sensation became around Sara's shoulders. "I hate to say this, but I don't think she's here."

"Only one way to find out, boss."

Sara rang the bell and sighed. "Let's see what this holds for us."

The answer was nothing. The door remained firmly closed. Barry peered through the front bay window and then contacted the others round the back. Craig revealed all was quiet with him and Carla as well. Sara opened the letterbox, but there was no sight or sound of her.

She left the small garden at the front and ran her finger down the sheet of paper to find the address of the woman who had called the station earlier. "It's the one over there."

They took several steps to the right, and then Sara rang the bell. A woman in her early sixties answered the door.

169

"Hello, I saw you leave your car. You're the police, aren't you?"

"That's right." Sara produced her ID. "Thank you for contacting us. I don't suppose you've seen Miss Lyle today, have you?"

"Oh, that's her name, is it? Yes, she went out about thirty minutes ago. Took all three children with her."

"Shit!" Sara cursed and then apologised. "Sorry, did you see which way she went? Was it by car or on foot?"

"Oh no, she took that car of hers. Went up the road, couldn't possibly tell you where she was heading."

"Can you give me any information about the car?"

"It's a medium-sized one, fairly new. Dark blue or black, that's as good as it gets, I'm afraid, dear. I've never been interested in the darn things. If my hubby was still around, he'd have all the information to hand for you. Unfortunately, he passed away over ten years ago. I miss the old sod but I'm coping all right on my own. I'm no longer a slave in the kitchen or doing the housework every day, not with only me here to make a mess."

Sara smiled, and her gaze was drawn in the direction the woman had pointed. "Not to worry. I'll let you get back to what you were doing."

"Watching TV, my only guilty pleasure these days."

Sara left the doorway and waved. "Ring the others, get them to join us, Barry."

They walked back to the car as he placed the call to Craig. It wasn't long before Carla and Craig appeared at the top of the alley. They seemed as disappointed as Sara.

"Another wasted trip, folks. The neighbour told us Lyle went out about thirty minutes ago, set off with the kids in the car."

"Took all the kids? Damn, that can only mean one thing…" Carla's voice trailed off.

Sara nodded. "Don't bother finishing off that sentence either. We still haven't got a clue what car she has."

"Someone around here must know," Craig suggested.

"You're right. We shouldn't give up at the first hurdle. Let's knock on a few doors, see if anyone is around who can give us a definitive answer."

They went back to Lyle's address and knocked on the doors closest to her house and asked the relevant question. One man gave Craig the answer they were hoping for. He rushed across the road and showed Sara the details in his notebook.

"Good job. Make and model and even the registration number. Something appears to be going our way, at last. Back to the station. Craig, call it in, see if we can pick the car up on any nearby ANPRs."

Craig got on the phone, and they sprinted back to the vehicles.

"You what?" Craig shouted from behind her.

Fear drew Sara to an immediate halt. She swiftly turned and demanded, "What's going on?"

"Jeff is receiving reports of an attempted child abduction on the edge of the city, down by Tesco."

"Get in the cars. We'll head over there now. Attempted?"

"Yes, the mother screamed, prevented the child from being taken, and two members of the public tackled the woman who tried to steal the kid."

"It must be her." Sara and her team dived back into the two vehicles and set off, sirens blaring. "Jesus, let's hope they've apprehended her."

"I wonder what she's done with the other three kids. If she only left the house half an hour ago, she must still have them with her, mustn't she?" Carla asked.

"Anything could have happened in that time. Until we

find out what her motive is, I don't think we should speculate."

Carla groaned. "Christ, you're right."

THEY ARRIVED at the supermarket car park to find a couple of patrol cars with four officers trying to keep the inquisitive crowd at bay. Sara left her car door open and ran towards the officers, the three other members of her team in hot pursuit.

Sara flashed her ID at the officer who appeared to be in charge. "Where's the mother? What about the child?"

"We've taken her inside. The baby is unharmed and with her, ma'am."

"And the kidnapper?"

"She got away. We were too late to stop her."

Sara scanned the crowd in the hope that she would recognise Lyle lingering amongst the members of the public, as some perps often did after the event. She couldn't see anyone who remotely looked like her, so she continued inside the supermarket with Carla to have a word with the mother. That left Craig and Barry helping the uniformed officers to disperse the crowd.

Inside, they found a woman sitting by the lift, two men standing behind her, and a pram with a screaming baby at her side. The mother was wheeling the pram back and forth in an attempt to pacify the little one.

Sara approached the woman and flashed her warrant card. "DI Sara Ramsey. How are you both?"

"Petrified. How would you feel if someone had tried to take a child in your care right from under your nose?" the young woman snapped in reply.

"Wait, this isn't your baby? What's your name?"

"No, I'm a child minder. Her mother is at work. I look after her for two and a half days a week. I'm Lena Johnson."

"I see, and you were here shopping?"

"Yes, I had a few essentials to pick up so that I could give the baby her lunch, some nibbles and some nappies."

"Can you tell me what happened?"

"I was pushing the pram across the car park when this woman drew up in a car alongside me."

Sara withdrew her phone from her pocket and showed Lena the picture of Fiona Lyle. "Is this her?"

"Yes, I would recognise her anywhere. Shit, it's just dawned on me, isn't that the woman whose face has been plastered over the TV screens? Is she the one stealing the kids? Christ, is that what this is all about? It didn't click with me at the time, all I could concentrate on was saving baby Annabel." She glanced back at the two men behind her. "If it hadn't been for Steve and Dan, she would have successfully driven off with the baby."

"Can you run through the events, step by step?"

"Yes, as I said, I was on my way to the supermarket. I was at the back of the car park when this woman stopped the car alongside me. She got out. The first thing I noticed was that she had other children in the vehicle with her. They were all crying; one was screaming as though there was something wrong with it, poor mite. I thought she was going to strike up a conversation with me, maybe ask for some advice, seeing how well-behaved Annabel was at the time. I smiled and said hi to her, and she returned the smile and peered into the pram. When she stood up again her expression had totally changed. It was dark, almost evil. Her eyes were blazing, and she snarled at me, told me to hand over the kid or she would kill me."

"What did you do?"

"I couldn't hand over Annabel. Connie, her mother would never forgive me. So I screamed at the top of my lungs, and these two lovely gents came to my rescue. Heroes, they are."

Sara looked at the men and nodded. "Thanks for your help, very courageous of you both. Did the kidnapper have a weapon?"

"She had a knife. I'm a martial arts expert. I showed her some moves to prove I wasn't afraid to tackle her, but she still managed to nick me with the knife. Steve was distracted, tried to lend a hand, and she got away from us. We both kicked ourselves. We had her in our grasp, and she got away."

"Don't worry. Can you confirm what type of car it was? We believe she's probably been stealing vehicles and then dumping them, doing her absolute best to put us off the scent."

"Yes, it was a navy-blue Ford Focus." Steve handed her a business card. On the back of it was written a registration number.

"Excellent. We'll get the word out about this before we go any further. Carla, can you sort that out for me?"

Carla took the card and stepped away to make the call to the station.

"Has the mother been informed, Lena?" Sara asked.

Ashamed, her chin dropped to her chest. "I couldn't call her. I tried but chickened out. I wouldn't know how to put it into words."

"I'll do it for you, she should know right away."

"I'm sorry."

Lena gave Sara the mother's mobile number.

Sara waited until Carla had returned before she left the group to make the call. "Hello, is that Connie?"

"It is. Who's this?"

"Hello, Connie, I'm DI Sara Ramsey. Please don't be alarmed. I want to assure you from the outset that both Annabel and Lena are okay."

"What? If they're okay then why is a police officer calling me? I don't understand. Tell me what's going on, now."

"We're down at Tesco in the city centre. We were alerted to an incident which occurred not long ago. It involved Lena and your daughter. They're safe and unharmed."

"I'm glad to hear it, but why are you skirting around the truth? I demand to know what's going on."

"Lena, along with two members of the public, prevented an attempted kidnapping."

"No! Are you telling me that someone tried to take my child? Oh God, you're not the one investigating all the child abductions that have taken place this week, are you?"

"Yes, that's me. They're okay. They're safe. This is merely a courtesy call to let you know that an incident took place. Lena was too upset to call you herself."

"But they're both okay?"

"Yes."

"And the person who tried to steal my baby? I hope you have them in custody."

"Sadly not. She got away."

"What the fuck? My God, this is terrible. What are you doing about this?"

"Our very best. Now that I've informed you of the incident, I'm going to need to crack on and find this woman before she gets too far away."

"I'd better let you go then. Tell Lena I'm going to tell my boss that I'm leaving. I should be there within twenty minutes."

"I was hoping you would say that. I'll pass on the message. You'll find them inside the main entrance."

"Of course I would be there for Annabel and Lena, what type of mother do you take me for?"

"I didn't mean to offend you. I'll pass the message on and get back to work. Thank you for accepting my call."

The line went dead, and Sara sighed heavily. On the walk back to the group, she ignored all the expletives under the sun fighting their way into her mouth. She smiled at Lena who appeared to be apprehensive about her return.

"Was she okay? Does she blame me?" Lena's voice quivered.

Sara shook her head. "No, she doesn't blame you, and yes, she's very relieved to hear that you're both safe. She's asking her boss if she can leave and should be here soon. Where does she work?"

"She works at the council, in the admin department. That's as much as I know, sorry."

"There's no need for you to apologise. How are you doing now?"

She held up a mug. "Better now I've got some caffeine pumping around my system." Tears bulged, and she wiped them with a tissue Carla handed to her. "I don't think I'll ever get over the thought of someone going out of their way to snatch Annabel. Out in the open like this and in the middle of the damn day, what's that all about? The nerve of that woman."

"I know it's going to be near impossible for you to get over, but you mustn't let it affect you in the future. Do that and she's won."

"Easy for you to say. It was horrendous. This has to be the worst day of my life. I can't imagine what I'd be like if Steve and Dan hadn't had the balls to jump in and help us."

"Don't worry about it. We couldn't sit back and let something like that happen, not to a baby. Who knows what that nutter's intentions might be?" Steve said. He glanced down at his blood-soaked sleeve.

"You need to get yourself off to hospital, or should I call an ambulance?" Sara asked.

"I'm fine, it's just a scratch. One of the first aiders around here cleaned it up for me. We both decided it wasn't worth a trip to A and E."

"I still think you should get it checked out in case there's a chance of infection."

"Okay, you win. Do you need a statement from us?"

"Not right now. I'll get one of the officers to take down all your details, and someone from the station will be in touch soon with a time and date that is suitable for you. Thanks again for stepping up to the plate, not everyone would have willingly got involved. I'm grateful for your intervention. I don't suppose you saw in which direction she went, did you?"

"I did," Dan said. "I watched her go around the round-about and head off down Victoria Street towards the river."

"Great news. We'll concentrate the search on that area. Are you going to be okay, Lena? Do you need us to wait with you until Connie gets here?"

"No. I'd rather you get after that bitch. I'm worried about the other kids she had in the car with her."

"That's my concern as well." Sara squeezed Lena's shoulder and shook Dan's and Steve's hands. "It's a pleasure meeting you both, thanks again for all you did. The press will be here soon, it's up to you whether you speak to them or not. Most people don't tend to hang around. But it's entirely up to you."

"I'm out of here, I'm late for a meeting as it is," Steve said.

"Yep, I've got better things to do with my time as well," Dan agreed.

"How are you feeling now, Lena?" Sara asked.

"I'm fine. I'll sit here until Connie comes."

Sara smiled, and she and Carla left the supermarket and rushed back to the car. Craig and Barry saw them coming and left the other officers to organise the crowd and joined them at Sara's vehicle.

"According to one of the witnesses, she went left on the

roundabout, towards the river. I suggest we drive around for a while, see what we can find."

"That's a busy part of town, boss, with several possible escape routes out of the city within easy reach."

"I'm aware of that. What's bugging me is her need to snatch another baby. Why? And is she about to try a second time?"

Craig ran a hand across his chin. "Hmm... I see what you mean, that's a distinct possibility."

"It is. Let's get on the road again. I'll call the station, get the area flooded with every available patrol car, it might freak her out and force her arm. If she's still in the area, of course."

The four of them climbed back in their cars, and Sara reversed to ease away from the milling crowd. She turned left at the roundabout with Craig and Barry close behind her.

Carla had brought up a map of Hereford on her phone, and together they ran through the different possibilities open to Fiona Lyle.

"It's impossible to second-guess her," Carla said. "Look at the number of routes she could take. She could be anywhere by now."

"Being defeatist about this is not going to help us, Carla."

"All I was trying to be was honest."

"I'm going to do a large sweep of the area. Keep your eyes open for her car, at least we know what it is now and the plate number. If anything, we should get a ping from the ANPRs soon enough."

Carla's crossed fingers shot in the air. "You'd hope that was the case."

Sara circled the area, taking several main roads out of the city centre before heading back into the city once more. Nothing came to light. About an hour later, they received a call they'd been waiting for. Lyle's car had been spotted by an observant member of the public who had alerted a passing patrol car. The man had informed them that a young woman appeared panic-stricken. He'd seen her getting out of the car with three screaming kids and had gone into the forest at Belmont Country Park.

Sara put her foot down. Carla called Craig and Barry, and they followed Sara through a shortcut that led them out to Belmont.

"It's a good job we were close to this road," Carla said. "If we'd been on the other side of the city, we would have been in trouble."

"Nice to think something is going in our favour for a change. I wonder what her objective is. Why take them into the forest?" No sooner had the words left her lips than vile images of child sacrifices filled Sara's mind. "Sometimes I wish I'd kept my mouth shut. You don't want to know what type of images I have going on in my head."

"I bet." Carla laughed. "Let's stick with what we know rather than dealing with what might happen."

"Thanks for the advice, partner."

Once they arrived at the location, they parked the cars next to Lyle's Ford Focus. Sara peeked through the window, making sure she hadn't left any of the children inside the vehicle. Craig and Barry, along with four uniformed officers, joined them a few minutes later. The team gathered around and decided it would be better initially to take the main route through the forest and see where that led them. Sara's pulse raced faster and harder the further they got into the dense forest. That was until the opening emerged ahead of them.

"Have you ever been here before?" she asked Carla.

"I have, years ago. There would be no point in you asking me where it leads because I wouldn't be able to tell you."

Sara paused and asked the others, "Anyone know this area well?"

The rest of the group shook their heads.

"Okay, then we'll stick with our original plan and see where this route leads us."

In fact, it led to a vast lake. There were trees on all sides. A path wound its way through the trees and around the lake. A couple walking two dogs were a few hundred yards ahead of them. Sara upped her pace to catch up with them.

"Hi, sorry to interrupt your leisurely stroll. I was wondering if you've passed a woman with three young children, either in a buggy or a pram perhaps."

"We saw her in the distance a while ago. She ventured into the wooded area over to the right. The babies were all crying, and she appeared to be losing her rag with them. Sorry if I'm speaking out of turn, years of experience talking. I'm a primary school teacher," the female said.

"Ah, that would explain it," Sara replied. "Over there, you say?" She pointed to the left at a large clump of trees beyond the lake.

"That's right. It wasn't too long ago. I saw she was struggling and I was about to offer her a hand, but hubby warned me to keep my distance."

"It's okay. Thanks for your help." Sara started to walk away but then returned to the couple. "Sorry, me again. I take it you know this area well, do you?"

"We come here every week to walk the dogs," the man confirmed. "Why?"

"Can you tell me where that path would likely come out?" Sara asked, her gaze drifting to the clump of trees. She was hopeless at getting her bearings in this type of environment.

"It doubles back to the car park but it also takes another route to yet another lake, a smaller one just beyond."

"Crap. Okay, thanks very much for all your help." Sara

returned to the rest of the group and explained what they needed to do next. "We're going to have to split up. Let's get to the crossroads, see what we're up against."

"We know she's a canny bitch, boss," Craig said. "I bet she's going to return to the car."

"That's what I'm thinking, why take the detour in the first place? Unless…" Sara quickly scanned the lake.

"No, you don't think she's come here to dump the babies, do you?" Carla asked.

"I wouldn't put it past her. She's already had a close shave today. What's to stop her feeling fed up and getting rid of the kids?"

"If we knew what her motive was for taking them in the first place, it might give us some insight into what's going on in that screwed-up head of hers," Carla said.

"Let's stick with the facts. She came here for a reason and brought the babies with her."

Carla's gaze immediately settled on the lake. "I can't see anything bobbing around on the surface. Christ, what if she's tied weights to their legs and thrown them in?"

"You have a vivid imagination that scares me at times, partner."

"Sorry, but why else would she come here? For a frantic stroll around the lake? The witness told us that she was stressed."

"Yep, okay. Standing around here weighing up the pros and cons of what she might be thinking isn't helping matters." Sara set off, and the others followed her.

When they reached the area the witness had advised Lyle had taken the children, Sara couldn't help herself, she ran to the water's edge to see if the lake was clear or if the bottom had been disturbed, muddying the waters. It hadn't. She let out a relieved sigh and continued to the end of the path where a signpost was situated. To the right was another walk and to the left was the way out.

"We need to split up. Craig and Barry, you take the longer route and take two officers with you, and you two come with me and Carla. Ring me as soon as you find anything."

The teams set off in the different directions. Sara noted how disturbed the path was becoming as the trees thinned out in the surrounding area. She found herself regretting not putting on a pair of wellies. The car was going to get filthy, and she saw a weekend of car-cleaning duties in her near future. The clearing opened out ahead of them.

Sara glanced over at her car and the gap sitting beside it. "Shit! She's bloody duped us again. She had all this planned. Giving us the runaround as and when she can. Fuck! What's she up to? And has she got the kids with her?"

There were a few other cars parked up but no one nearby whom they could speak to.

"Get on the phone to Craig, Carla. Tell them to make their way back to the cars. I'm going to call the station, get this area flooded. We neither have the time nor the manpower to search every inch of this area. We need to get on the road again."

"What's she bloody up to?" Carla said, her fist striking her thigh.

"Your guess is as good as mine."

CHAPTER 9

"Why are you ringing me?" Fiona asked her contact.

"Because I've got the families coming down heavily on me, demanding to know why I haven't delivered the kids yet. If there is still a deal to be done, I want to start over and give you what you want," Liz replied.

Fiona grinned, she knew her contact would come running back to her with time at a premium. *She needs me as much as I need her, if not more. Time to see how far I can push her, after her sending those louts to try and kill me.* Her temper raged at the thought. "I told you, pay the extra and I might consider the deal back on the table, if not, I've been in contact with a group willing to take the kids off my hands." She paused to let that snippet of information sink in for a second. "They'll be transporting them out of the country, so no chance of it backfiring on me, unlike your proposition."

"What? You can't do that, what sort of life will those kids get?"

"Like you and I give a shit about that. It's too late for you to suddenly develop a conscience. You know my terms, and that means you sticking to your side of the bargain and not sending another lot of tossers to rob the kids. As you can see, I can more than look after myself. I bet that was a shocker, wasn't it, knowing that I can often give as good as I get?"

"There was no need to kill him, he was valuable to me."

"Then why send him? His death was down to you and your inability to trust me. What kind of working relationship is that? You know what? I'm sticking to my new plan, it's obvious you have little to no respect for me."

"Wait! No, that's not true. The fact is, I underestimated you. I admit I treated you appallingly."

"Now what? You regard us more as partners?"

"I wouldn't go that far. Let's just say I appreciate the value you have contributed to the deal."

"Pity you didn't value it in the first instance, instead of trying to shaft me, in more ways than one. So, what about the money?"

"You can have your ten grand."

"When? Where?"

"I'll deposit it in your account after you deliver the kids."

"You think I was born yesterday? That ain't going to happen."

"All right, if you've got a better proposition, let's hear it," Liz replied.

Fiona sensed the other woman's anxiety and frustration in her tone. "You meet me, I deliver the kids, and you hand over the cash at the same time."

"I don't do kids. I wouldn't know how to handle them or see to their needs," Liz objected, her voice escalating a couple of octaves.

"And yet it was okay for you to expect me to be able to deal with them, with no bloody experience behind me."

"You volunteered. I didn't force you into doing anything

you weren't willing to do. We're going over old ground here, when we should be trying to resolve the issue."

"I've told you what needs to happen. You meet me and we'll do the exchange. What you do after that ain't my problem."

"All right. Name a time and place and I'll be there."

"Alone. Don't go bringing any of your goons with you either. Start treating me with respect, got that?"

"I've got it, I promise, nothing underhand will happen, you have my word. I've got the cash here. Tell me where."

Fiona paused again, this time to weigh up her options. She should meet out in the open, that way Liz would be less likely to have her muscle pounce on her. "The racecourse, main entrance, be there at four, on the dot."

"Are you sure? There will probably be lots of people around at that time of day, especially if the weather is good."

"And that's exactly why I suggested it."

"Oh, right. Okay. I'll be there."

Fiona ended the call. Now all she had to do was keep the coppers off her tail for the next couple of hours. The question was, did she have it in her to try and snatch the final baby? The last attempt had been a huge mistake. Was Liz expecting four babies? She hadn't mentioned the number over the phone, and there lay a huge dilemma.

CHAPTER 10

*D*efeated, the team returned to the station. The damn woman had gone to ground, leaving them clueless where to look next for her. Sara had ordered the search of Belmont Park. While she eagerly awaited the outcome, she paced the incident room, driving Carla nuts.

"That's not helping," Carla mumbled as Sara walked past her desk for the umpteenth time since their return.

"It's all I've got at the moment. How did she get away from us? Why aren't the damn cameras doing their job and picking her up?"

"Because she's clever, we've already established that much."

Sara flung her hands in the air. "Yeah, I know. But we need to find a way of getting one step ahead of her if we want to save those kids."

"We could get a search warrant for her house. Tear it apart, looking for clues. She must have taken them somewhere, she must have. What if she's swapped cars by now? How the heck are we going to find her?" Craig asked.

Carla pointed a finger. "To do that, she'd have to visit one of the dealerships in the area. We could do the rounds, ring them, warn them what's likely to happen."

Sara shrugged. "We could, but is she really going to do that? Buy from a dealership when her face has been plastered all over the news?"

"You've got a point. Okay, if *we're* thinking along those lines then she must have considered it as well."

"We're back to square one." Sara kicked out at a nearby chair. It flew across the room and clattered into a desk on the other side. "One thing, one sighting, that's all we need. It isn't too much to bloody ask, is it? What about the witnesses at the lake? The woman said she didn't like the way Lyle was treating the children, and yet she didn't bloody call the police, did she? Lyle's image has been plastered all over the screens, and still people are doing bugger all about it. What's the point in holding these conferences?"

"You mustn't think that way. We do benefit from them during most investigations, just not this one. Why? I really couldn't tell you."

"Which is ultimately the frustrating part, isn't it?"

IT WASN'T until later on that day that their hopes rose a notch. Craig and Barry were doing their thing with the cameras when Craig shouted that he'd got something.

"Here, boss. Coming out of the Premier Inn car park."

Sara peered over his shoulder at the enhanced image. "That's her. Can we track where she's heading? What about the number plate, is it visible?"

"I've checked, it's different to the one she had before, that's how she's managed to avoid the cameras. We've got her now, though, boss."

"Carla, I think we should get out there. Craig, I know how much you enjoy being out in the field, however, I'd prefer it if you stayed here. You're more use to me tracking her movements on the camera."

"I agree, boss. It's fine by me."

"Marissa, grab your jacket, I want you to go with Barry. We've got more chance of trapping her if there are two vehicles out there. Let's go!"

"Good luck," Jill shouted as the four of them headed out of the door.

"You, too. Give it your all, guys. Don't let her slip through our fingers again."

SARA KEPT in touch with Craig during their trip out to where Lyle had last been seen. He told her that the car appeared to be going around in circles, taking different routes that ended back at the same spot, the Premier Inn.

"What the heck is she playing at?" Sara muttered, more to herself than to Carla or Craig, who was still on the line.

"Maybe she's trying to settle the babies down," Carla offered as a suggestion. "Isn't that supposed to be a way to pacify kids?"

"Is it? I wouldn't know," Sara replied. "Okay, Craig, we're here now. We'll tuck the car into the Beefeater restaurant next door and tail her if she shows up."

"Sounds like a plan," Craig said. "How far are you from the location, boss?"

"We're coming up to Dunelm now, so not far at all."

"Okay, there's no sign of her at the moment. I'm going to flick around the cameras in that area. I'll give you a shout once I've located her."

Sara ended the call and indicated left into the Beefeater car park. She reversed into a slot that gave her good visibility to the adjacent Premier Inn. Barry parked in the space next to hers, awaiting further instructions.

"Let's hope we can grab her soon, those kids must be frantic by now," Carla said.

"And driving her around the twist, that's my main concern. She could snap, if she's not used to having kids around, to suddenly end up being in charge of three of them."

"Christ, it doesn't bear thinking about. I bet I'm right, that's why she's driving round and round, in the hope it keeps them quiet."

"More than likely. We just need a break, one tiny break, so we can pounce on her and rescue the kids. However, we need to be as crafty as her."

"She's got the upper hand, or so it would seem," Carla said with a shrug.

Sara's mobile rang. "She's coming up to B and Q now, boss, you should see her shortly."

Her gaze shifted to the main entrance, and there she was. "I've got her."

Sara gesticulated to get Barry's attention and pointed at Lyle's car. He gave her the thumbs-up and lowered his window.

"Keep your eyes open, Barry, we'll follow her the next time she makes a move, but at a distance."

"Will do, boss."

Sara watched the woman fidget in the car. Every now and again she peered over her shoulder. Occasionally, she knelt in the front seat and pointed her finger at the babies in the back.

"She's getting hot under the collar, as though she's ready to explode. Why has she got the kids? Does she intend to palm them off? Is that why she's circling the area?"

"Possibly, otherwise, wouldn't she take them somewhere else? She knows going back to her place isn't an option open to her."

189

"That reminds me. Get onto the station, ask Jill to chase up the search warrant for her address."

Carla made the call while Sara kept her gaze trained on Lyle. The woman kept placing her head in her hands and then lashing out at the steering wheel, making Sara feel more and more uneasy about what she was liable to do next.

"Shit, she's becoming unstable, to my trained eye," she said when Carla ended the call.

"I've been watching her. I think you're right. Would it be worth pulling up alongside her, making our move now?"

"I was wondering the same. Wait, she's started the engine. Sit tight, we're on the move." Sara turned to face Barry.

He'd already noticed and crept forward.

Sara gave Lyle a few metres' clearance and then followed her onto the main road. She caught the tail end of her car taking a left at the roundabout. Sara sat at the busy junction for a second or two, to allow a couple of cars to get between her and Lyle. Barry kept with her.

"Keep an eye on her, Carla. Tell me if she indicates or takes an unexpected turn. I'm far enough back for her not to detect me."

"I'm on it. So far so good." Carla pointed. "Hang on, she's taking a left, left, left, into the racecourse."

"Interesting. Is there a play area in there for the kids?"

"What are you asking me for? As if I'd know."

"All right, there's no need to snap at me. I'll indicate well in advance to let Barry know."

Barry responded by issuing another thumbs-up.

Sara's heart raced and thumped against her ribs. "I'm going to see if I can block her exit."

"How can you say that if you're not sure about the area?"

"All right. It was just a thought. She's pulled up. There are a few other cars around, probably dog walkers, out here exercising their hounds. Wait, she seems keen on keeping an eye on that car on the right. There's a woman inside." Sara fell quiet as she watched the proceedings.

"I'm sensing they know each other. What if they're about to make the switch?"

"I'm getting the same impression. Get backup here ASAP, Carla. Tell them to approach quietly, no sirens."

While Carla rang the station and spoke to the desk sergeant to make the arrangements, Sara contacted Barry to bring him up to speed on what she thought was about to go down.

"What do you want me to do, boss, sit tight?" Barry asked.

"For the time being. As soon as I leave the car, I want you to do the same. Hopefully backup will be with us by then."

"Okay, boss."

Sara observed Lyle get out of the car and stop in between the two vehicles. "I think the exchange is definitely about to take place. It seems like neither woman is prepared to give an inch. Lyle has stopped equidistance to both cars."

Carla ended the call. "They'll be here in five minutes or less, depending on the traffic. If this is the drop-off, isn't it a bit out in the open?"

"Definitely. Maybe that's Lyle's intention. Perhaps there's a trust issue going on here."

"Money at stake will do that to the best of people, I guess."

"Too right. The other woman is now leaving her vehicle and she's got a large carrier bag with her."

"Loaded with cash, no doubt," Carla said.

Neither woman filled Sara with the sense that she cared two hoots about the kids. The new arrival was dressed in a smart suit with a skirt just above the knees and four-inch stilettos.

"Does she seem the motherly type to you?" Sara asked.

"Nope. Not in the slightest. If she's buying the kids from

Lyle, maybe the other one is a go-between and will be selling the kids on to someone else."

"Christ, don't say that, although watching what's going down, I think you're probably right." Sara anxiously glanced in her rear-view mirror, willing the backup teams to arrive, and quickly. She was itching to get out there. From what she could see, neither woman was carrying a weapon, not that it would matter if they were out of the car and away from the children. "I'm making the call. Backup or not, I've got to get in there."

Sara pushed open the car door and got out. Barry, Carla and Marissa did the same, closing the doors of the cars quietly so as not to draw attention to themselves. One more glance over her shoulder, and Sara let out a relieved sigh when two patrol cars entered the car park. She beckoned the officers to join them, and together, the group approached the two women who were oblivious to what was going on around them.

Sara gestured for Marissa and Carla to get closer to the Ford so they could swoop for the children before Lyle could reach them.

Once her two colleagues were in position, Sara shouted, "Police. Fiona Lyle, you're under arrest for kidnapping three children."

Lyle turned swiftly and withdrew a knife from the back of her jeans. Sara hadn't been prepared for that and cursed herself for not having her Taser drawn and ready to use. The other woman screamed. Lyle hooked an arm around her throat and stuck the blade to the other woman's throat.

Shit, that's not how I planned it. Now I'm going to have to bargain with this nutter and probably put the babies at risk all over again.

"Please, you have to help me," the smartly dressed woman

pleaded. She tottered on her heels, the gravel moving beneath her feet.

Sara raised her hands. "Let's keep this nice and calm. Lyle, you're surrounded, there's no escaping the area. We have the babies now. Let the woman go and give yourself up."

"Fuck off. You think I'm going to listen to a word you say? You're a crap detective, admit it, I've led you up so many garden paths throughout this investigation, you haven't got a clue what's going on, have you?"

"I admit that you're a very convincing woman who has probably had the upper hand throughout, but that's no longer the case. Let her go, and we can discuss this down at the station, Lyle."

She laughed. "It took you a while to figure out my real name."

"Please do something to help me, don't just stand there and let her get away with this."

"What's your part in this?" Sara asked, determined to find out the truth while Lyle was holding a knife to the woman's throat.

"Yeah, enlighten the inspector as to the part you've played in all this, Liz." Lyle nicked Liz's throat. Blood dripped onto the collar of her pink silk blouse.

"I... umm... I can't," Liz stuttered.

"Then I'll fill the inspector in if you're refusing to do it. She got in touch with me, with instructions to abduct the babies. I would need to hold them, feed and change them, a massive chore to someone with my abilities to care for kids, which amounts to zero, let me tell you. Her job was to find families who would be willing to pay for the sprogs. Rich families who can't have kids of their own."

"You're a go-between?" Sara asked. Any sympathy she had for this woman dipped into oblivion.

"That's right, isn't it, Liz?" Lyle said, nicking her throat with the blade a second time.

Sobbing, Liz said, "Yes, without me, none of this would have materialised. I'm to blame, she's not. There, I've said it, you can let me go now."

"Ah, I would if you meant it. If I were to set you free, you'd probably say you made the declaration under duress, wouldn't you?" Lyle said. She tightened her hold, causing Liz to choke.

"All right, Fiona, you've made your point. Tell me where the babies were going to end up."

"In this country. I told her she should have sent them abroad, but she treated me like an idiot most of the time. Even sent two goons to snatch the babies from me because she thought I'd become a liability."

"And were you? It must have been hard taking care of the kids twenty-four hours a day. You've been under pressure all week, haven't you?"

Lyle laughed. "Yeah, you're right, but not as much as you. I bet your DCI is livid with you for being forced to plead to the public the number of times you've had to this week. How often does that happen, eh?"

"Never. Once is usually enough, so you can pat yourself on the back for deceiving us the way you have, over a long period. Maybe Liz wasn't the only one to have underestimated your abilities, Fiona."

"Too right. I've got brains, and it's about time people began treating me with a modicum of respect."

"Absolutely, and I'm about to do that, Fiona. Why don't you tell me what you're hoping to achieve next?"

"You're going to let me go and arrest her. She's the main 'woman' you're after. I was only carrying out instructions—to the letter, I might add."

"We can do that, if you hand her over to us."

Sara took a tentative step forward, but Fiona backed away a little, taking Liz with her and adding another nick to her already scratched throat at the same time. "Stop treating me like an idiot, Inspector."

Sara held her hands up again. "I wouldn't dream of it, I swear. Let her go, Fiona, I promise she will be arrested and charged for the kidnappings."

"Yeah, and what about me? All I was doing was carrying out her orders. She's the one who messed me around, tried to bump me off when things became unpredictable."

"I believe you, Fiona. Drop the knife, and we can discuss it down at the station. Give me a chance to put this right."

"Like I'm about to trust you. You coppers are all the same, you set out to get people onside and then bam… you invariably do a number on them. Lure them into a false sense of security as my old man used to say."

"Not at all. You have my word. If you're willing to work with me, we can get Liz banged up, but only if you agree to work with me. Together, we can put her away for a long time."

"And you're willing to cut a deal with me?"

"Yes, on one proviso."

"Here we go. I should have known you'd try to pull a fast one. What?"

"You let us take the kids now."

"No way. They're my ticket out of here. I haven't gone through a nightmare of a week only to hand them over before I've received my compensation."

Sara shrugged. "Then we're at an impasse, Fiona. The ball is in your court."

"Don't listen to her. She's as much at fault as I am. Yes, I might have come up with the original idea, but then the plan grew and grew because of her input," Liz said out of the blue.

Sara winced. The woman was either brave or foolish to

be that outspoken when someone was holding a knife to her throat with evil intent flowing through their veins.

Angry, Fiona yanked Liz's head back with her free hand and exposed the length of her throat. Sara sensed this was the beginning of the end.

"I'm not taking the fall for this," Fiona said. "If you're not going to take me seriously, then I have no other option left but to kill"

Both women fell forward after a heavy force hit them from behind. Sara leapt in, reached for Liz's arm and pulled the woman towards her. At the same time, Fiona ended up facedown on the gravel with Craig straddling her back, the knife she'd been holding at Liz's neck lying a few feet away.

Sara smiled appreciatively at Craig. "I'm so glad you didn't follow orders on this one, Craig. Good man."

He nodded and said, "I couldn't sit there, watching events unfold through the drone. I had to come down here and give you a hand, ma'am."

"Great job, you're always working on your initiative. I've said it before, you're going to go far in your career. Take them in, guys."

The uniformed officers cuffed and removed the two women, putting them in separate cars for the journey back to the station.

Sara took the time to pat Craig on the back and said, "Between you and me, I must admit, I couldn't see how that one was going to end, so I'm super grateful for your inter-vention." She wagged her finger. "But don't put your life at risk like that again, you hear me?"

"I won't, I promise. I knew I was safe. I took a punt it was the right time to jump her once she exposed the other woman's neck like that. I presumed there was only going to be one outcome."

"I believe you read the situation well, considering you

were viewing the events from behind. Now get back to the station, we've got lots of work to do yet before we wrap this case up."

"Rightio, boss. On my way."

The babies cried, and it brought Sara back down to earth with a bang. She rushed over to Marissa and Carla who were each jiggling a babe in their arms. Sara reached into the back seat and removed the third baby and awkwardly held the crying bundle of joy.

"We'd better get onto social services, let them deal with the children. They'll probably need to get checked over at the hospital, but let SS deal with that, we've got enough to do back at the station. We'll need to ring all the parents as well, let them know the children are safe. First step is to get them back to the station, I think. We've never had to deal with rescuing babies before, have we?"

"I believe what you've just laid out is correct. How are we going to transport them safely back to the station?"

"I'll ring Jeff, tell him to send another squad car for one of the babies, then you can hold one in the back of my car and Marissa can do the same in Barry's."

"Great!" Carla's nose wrinkled. "Eew... I think this one needs changing."

Marissa dipped her head closer to the baby she was holding and nodded. "Yes, that makes two of them."

Sara suppressed the laugh threatening to emerge and walked away to place the call to social services to check what the proper procedure would be. Once she'd rung SS and told her colleagues the children would be collected from the station within the hour, Sara made the call to return to base before she contacted the parents. There was a lingering doubt in her mind whether the parents had a right to know at this early stage because the main question jumping up and down in her head was if they had discovered the right babies.

With the cars loaded and the babies more settled than they had been fifteen minutes before, they returned to the station. Sara caught Carla watching her in the rear-view mirror.

"What's going on in that head of yours? I can tell you're distracted about something. What is it?" her partner asked.

"What if there are more babies out there? What if these babies don't belong to the parents who have contacted us? What if we hand them back and they turn out to be someone else's babies?"

"That's why we need to get social services involved. I'm sure they won't hand the babies back willy-nilly. We'll leave them to sort it out, we'll pass on all the photos of the babies and let them deal with it."

"Yes, yes, you're right."

Sara fell quiet. This case had taken a lot out of her, to the extent she now found herself questioning her every move.

As if reading her thoughts, Carla said, "Stop it. Relax, we've rescued them. That's the end of the line for us. Now the responsibility lies with someone else."

"Yeah, you're right. I'm still going to need to call the parents, though. It wouldn't feel right keeping them out of the loop at this stage. Not when the media is likely to air the story soon after getting the news from one of their sources."

"Yes, that's the right thing to do before we interview Lyle and the other woman, Liz. I'm not sure about her, are you?"

"She's as much at fault as Lyle. I'm going to ensure the CPS are aware of that, too. The question is, whether this is their first venture or if there have been others over the years. I think it's the first they've carried out together, but who knows what they've got up to in the past?"

"True enough. I got the impression that Liz is going to be a willing interviewee, not sure if the same can be said for Lyle. I guess time will tell."

. . .

THE PARENTS WERE all overjoyed to hear the news, as expected, but they were far from happy to be told that it would be a few days yet before the children could be returned to them. But that part was out of Sara's hands.

DCI Price summoned her before the interviews began.

"I wanted to congratulate you and your team on a job well done, Sara, I know and appreciate how difficult this investigation has been for everyone. You've stuck with it and given it your all throughout."

Sara shrugged. "It was a challenge, ma'am, but we came good in the end. I'll pass on your congratulations to the team."

Carol Price cleared her throat. Sara got the impression that there was something else she needed to get off her chest.

"Was there anything else, boss?"

"Yes, I'm not sure how to say this."

"I always find it's best not to think about it too much, just to come out with it."

"That's because you're a wise lady, Sara Ramsey. I'm thrilled to have you part of my team, you know that…"

"I sense a *but* coming."

"But… I believe you're in desperate need of a break. When was the last time you had any decent time off?"

"Gosh, now you're testing me. I think it was back in the autumn. I must admit, it's tempting, however, there's far too much to do around here regarding this investigation."

Carol smiled. "Nothing that can't be put on hold or passed on to your partner for a week or so."

Sara cringed at the thought of breaking that snippet of news to Carla. "I'll make a deal with you, give me two, three days tops, to break the back of the paperwork on this investigation, and then I'll consider taking a week off."

Price extended her hand across the table and Sara shook it. "That's a deal."

"Wait, aren't you supposed to be taking time off soon yourself?"

"I can postpone it, if necessary, your need is greater than mine. You're no use to me out there if you're not firing on all cylinders. Before you snap my head off, I'm not saying you were guilty of slacking on this case either. You know what I mean, we all need to recharge our batteries from time to time. Will Mark be able to get time off?"

"That's another stumbling block. I'm not sure, his practice is getting busier and busier."

"Can't he call on an agency to help out for the week?"

"Leave it with me, I'll see what I can do. Thanks for thinking of me, boss. I'd better get on, I have two suspects to interview."

"I hope you're not going to hold them at the same time."

"No, I might ask Craig and Barry to interview one of them."

Price winked at her. "You really ought to delegate more, that's a good call. Now get out of here."

"I'm going. I'll let you know, if and when, I decide to take a week off."

"No, that's a definite *when*, and make it soon."

THE INTERVIEWS WENT BETTER than anticipated. Sara handed the reins over to Craig and Barry to interview Fiona Lyle while she and Carla tackled Liz, whom Sara regarded as the more dangerous of the two women.

"How did you get involved with Fiona?" she asked.

Liz twisted her mug of coffee on the table and avoided looking at Sara when possible. "Through a contact. And no, I'm not revealing who that is."

Sara shrugged. "If that's how you want to play it. We've got a search warrant for your premises, we're bound to come across all the information regarding these illegal transactions soon."

"Whatever. You might as well work for your money."

"Oh, I do, don't worry about that. I work extremely hard to combat manipulative, scheming, conniving people like you. How many times have you made arrangements to abduct children to sell them on?"

"No comment."

During the rest of the interview, Sara hit a brick wall. She agreed to call time on it after another mind-numbing two hours. Leaving the room, she called Craig out of the other interview to check how he was getting on with Lyle. She had been far more open with him and constantly pointed the finger at Liz Short, blaming her for pulling the deal together and 'forcing her', as Lyle put it, to carry out the deed. But that's as far as it went with regard to finding the families involved in stumping up the cash for the babies. Therefore, they'd be reliant on what details materialised during the search of Liz's premises.

"Okay, let's call it a day. We'll sling them in a cell and see if they're more cooperative during the second round of interviews tomorrow."

Craig smiled and reentered the interview room.

Carla returned Liz to the cell and met Sara at the bottom of the stairs. "I don't know about you, but I'm shagged, and yes, I rarely use that word."

Sara laughed. "I know that feeling. Let's go home."

EPILOGUE

Sara got home that evening and collapsed onto the sofa. Misty jumped onto her lap for a cuddle. Mark found them snuggled up and asleep an hour or so later. He woke Sara blowing on her face and with a glass of wine in his hand.

"Hey, tough day?"

"Tough week. I'm knackered. I'm so sorry, I had every intention of getting on with the dinner, but as soon as I sat down, my eyelids started drooping."

He bent down and kissed her on the tip of the nose. "You look done in. Why don't we ring for a takeaway and just chill out for the evening? I'm cream-crackered, too."

"Here, take a seat, I'll sort out the menu and we can decide what we want."

Mark held up a hand. "No, stay there, I'll fetch it."

They chose a couple of dishes off the local Indian's menu, and Mark rang through the order then sat next to her and placed his head on her shoulder.

"I must be getting old. This week has really taken it out of me," Mark said.

"If you're old then I'm ancient. How are you fixed over the next few weeks?"

He raised his head and narrowed his eyes. "Why? What did you have in mind?"

"I've been ordered to take time off by DCI Price. I was wondering, if you could spare the time, perhaps we could go away for a week."

He closed his eyes. "I'm just running through my appointments in my head for the next couple of weeks, and there's nothing in there that I can't put on hold for a week or so, I'm sure the owners won't mind. Where did you have in mind?"

"I'm not sure. I don't think I want the hassle of spending hours at the airport, do you?"

"Why don't we hire a camper van and head up to the Lakes? We could even take this one with us." He stroked Misty under the chin.

"Could we? What about all that driving?"

"We'll share it, if we have to. Shall I look into it?"

"We'll do it tonight. How exciting, having a holiday to look forward to."

"I'll need to check my appointments before I give a definitive answer."

"Sounds good to me."

They raised their glasses and chinked them together.

"To us and our precious time exploring. I've always wanted to visit the Lakes," Sara said.

He leaned in for a kiss. "It will be wonderful, spending time with each other, in such a beautiful part of the world, with no interruptions. Shall we leave our phones at home?"

"Gosh, now there's a thought."

They shared another kiss, and Sara breathed out a relieved sigh.

Something to definitely look forward to. What could possibly go wrong?

. . .

THE END

THANK you for reading Evil Intent, Sara and Carla's next adventure can be found here The Games People Play

Have you read any of my fast paced other crime thrillers yet? Why not try the first book in the award-winning Justice series Cruel Justice here.

OR THE FIRST book in the spin-off Justice Again series, Gone In Seconds.

WHY NOT TRY the first book in the DI Sam Cobbs series, set in the beautiful Lake District, To Die For.

PERHAPS YOU'D PREFER to try one of my other police procedural series, the DI Kayli Bright series which begins with The Missing Children.

OR MAYBE YOU'D enjoy the DI Sally Parker series set in Norfolk, Wrong Place.

OR MY GRITTY police procedural starring DI Nelson set in Manchester, Torn Apart.

. . .

OR MAYBE YOU'D like to try one of my successful psychological thrillers <u>She's Gone</u>, <u>I KNOW THE TRUTH</u> or <u>Shattered Lives.</u>

KEEP IN TOUCH WITH M A COMLEY

Pick up a FREE novella by signing up to my newsletter today.
https://BookHip.com/WBRTGW

BookBub
www.bookbub.com/authors/m-a-comley

Blog

http://melcomley.blogspot.com

Why not join my special Facebook group to take part in monthly giveaways.

Readers' Group

Printed in Great Britain
by Amazon

27647794R00126